PRAISE FOR STAR TREK: TITAN: SWORD OF DAMOCLES

...one of the best-written Star Trek novels of the past couple years. Thorne takes these characters and creates realistic and interesting ones that I want to know more about. So much so that I was disappointed that the novel was not longer. – JEFF AYERS, TREKWEB. COM

...marks its author as one to watch in coming years– DREAMWATCH MAGAZINE

PRAISE FOR GEOFFREY THORNE'S SHORT FICTION

...Thorne's writing style makes for an entertaining read. To add to the almost noir-like atmosphere he pours on the similes and metaphors like syrup over a steaming fresh stack of blueberry pancakes. – THE NEW PODLER REVIEW OF BOOKS

... so good it warranted a change of protocol... and I'm glad I did! ...a thoroughly enjoyable story and one which I highly recommend – BEST SCIENCE FICTION STORIES. COM

BETTER ANGELS

a gray harbor novel by
GEOFFREY THORNE

THE WINTERMAN PROJECT

ISBN-13: 978-0615689395
ISBN-10: 0615689396
PRINTED IN THE UNITED STATES OF AMERICA

FOR SUSAN
this is your fault

PAPERS, PLEASE

Hi.

Welcome. If you know me, or, I suppose, my work, you'll find the journey you're about to take unfamiliar.

Normally I tell the stories of dragons and vampires or wizards or aliens. It's what I do and I like it.

If you know me, you probably like it too so this is a bit of a warning.

There will be no magical escapes here. There will be no amazing displays of super technology. This isn't that kind of story. Gray Harbor isn't that kind of place.

Which isn't to say there aren't monsters here and you'll definitely spend some time peeking into shadowed corners.

And there is, I guess, a quest of sorts but, like I said, I'm warning you. If you know me.

This is a story but it's not a fantasy.

If you don't know me, welcome; welcome to Gray Harbor, USA.

If you're a city-dweller– and the U.S. census says it's likely you are– you will find the Harbor familiar. Some of you may think you've even been there and that Gray Harbor is me not-very-cleverly concealing Detroit's identity or, maybe, Chicago's.

Let me put your mind at ease: No.

Like most of the good things in my work, Gray Harbor was born in a conversation I had with my wife. She had refused to read something- something with a haunted house, I think, and I'd had enough.

"You have to read it," I told her. "You're my wife, for God's sake. How will it look if you never read any of my stuff?"

"I don't like hobbits," she said (never mind that I don't write hobbits. That's some other guy.) "I like your writing but, every time someone pulls out a magic wand or talks to their cyborg buddy, I get sleepy."

Yes. It's true. We're in what used to be called a mixed marriage. I'm a geek and she's, well, whatever the opposite of a geek is.

"When you write something *real*, I'll read it."

Real. Wow. Well, I was pretty pissed, let me tell you. All my stories are real. That's the point of them. But, after I cooled down, I thought about it and, as usual, she was mostly right.

Sometimes the monsters can be like a crutch. Story getting dull? Just toss in a dragon, right? Sure. I could see her point.

Okay. But, of course, not being a writer herself, she falls into the trap that most civilians do: thinking writers get to choose the stories they write. Maybe some do or they say they do but I think they lie. The stories choose us and that's the truth of it.

After that talk I was on fire to write something to show I didn't need the crutch but nothing came. Nothing worth showing or talking about. It was all trite, just mishmashes of stuff I was watching on TV or had read elsewhere.

I wasn't in those stories and I thought, I knew, when she said real, she meant she wanted me to open a vein.

She wanted the truth.

But I couldn't do it.

That's the bottom line.

The stories that came to me then were the same sort that always had. For years. She'd humor me, read a few pages now and then, but the INSTANT an alien or undergod showed up I watched her eyes go dull.

Then, one day, I heard a lady covering a song by Marvin Gaye on the radio. I won't say which one here but some of you might guess it when you get to the end of this yarn.

Anyway, I heard it and, by the time it was done, I had Gray Harbor and all the stories in Gray Harbor crammed in my head. Pretty soon I was writing.

Good thing? That's up to you.

So this story is the child of an argument with my wife and Marvin Gaye's music; it's big and dark and unwieldy and mean and it's about as real as I get.

But there are monsters in it too, the kind you can actually meet.

Cheers.

GT – Los Angeles 2011

"Oh my god, Oh my god. Let me say about these cities, right. These American fucking cities. We saw a shed of them this tour. Some of them, they're all bright and shiny, still reaching up, still following the Kennedy plan or the Reagan plan or somebody's plan from way back, but they're reaching. Still. But these others. No. No, no, no, no. The opposite. Dead scary. It's like they're these huge fucking animals, like dinosaurs, y'know? And they, like, eat and kill and fuck until the food source, whatever it is, goes away or the comet hits or whatever. The axis shifts. And then they die, right, but, like, SLOW, like super slow. It's like they're so big it takes their brains, maybe, decades, maybe a hundred years, to realize they're sitting in a corpse." – Claire Aprillo – from **ON A CLAIRE DAY**, the interview in HEART OF ROCK MAGAZINE, October 2011

TRACK 1: TWISTIN' THE NIGHT AWAY

Nicky woke up in the dark and remembered...

...the cinderblock fists hammering down on him without mercy...

...the stench of imported bourbon, mixing like a comfortable lover with the rough but enticing aroma of authentic Cuban cigars...

...the coarse implacable feel of the burlap as his body thudded into the trunk...

He remembered the lid coming down.

There was music drifting in from somewhere- the car's radio, he guessed.

Somebody was listening to Sam Cooke.

Probably Gregor, he thought. *Stanis hates that 1960s shit.* The thought was involuntary, discordantly normal under the circumstances. The incongruity scared him back to business.

They hadn't tied him and he was grateful for that. They hadn't killed him either but it remained to be seen whether or not that was something to be happy about. There were plenty of things worse than a bullet in the face. He had a good little while to tally up a list of the worst before he realized the car was stopping.

Oh shit, he thought. *This is it.*

He heard and sort of felt the asphalt change to gravel and smelled, he thought, the hint of water, lots of water, over the engine exhaust. He hoped it wasn't the docks. God damn, he really hoped it wasn't that.

The docks meant privacy and privacy meant somebody wanted time with him. Fuck, the docks meant- well- pain was what they meant. Lots of pain, lots of time to feel it and nobody to hear his screams or care if they did.

The car stopped finally, the engine sputtering down to silence. Nicky didn't like that. The dwindling noise reminded him too much of his own future prospects. His body tensed as he heard the car doors open and slam shut. He started to sweat then, much to his own chagrin.

What a little bitch he was turning out to be. He'd always fancied himself the best sort of criminal: cool under pressure, quick with his hands and way too smart to ever get caught by anybody, much less other crooks.

Even if somebody did catch him doing something dirty, even if he knew his number was up, he always thought he'd go down like a fucking man. Not like this. Not dripping with fear sweat. Not fighting to keep from pissing himself before anybody even laid a hand.

Somebody, Stanis it sounded like, said something in something that wasn't English.

There was a noise of keys in the trunk lock and then the hood came up above him. There were two shadows hanging there, silhouetted by the single yellowed street lamp.

One was thin and shrouded in a haze of blue smoke; the other massive and humming some disjointed tune.

Nicky was grateful for the silhouettes. The last

things he needed right then were Gregor's concrete gargoyle face grinning down at him like the fucking King of Pain or Stanis' hatchet-carved features and empty, glassy eyes lasering through him.

Fuck that.

Listening to Gregor stumbling over whatever ditty that was supposed to be was plenty bad enough.

Twisting the Night Away. Was that the song Gregor was looking for? Jesus.

Jesus Christ, thought Nicky. *I'm so fucking dead. I'm so dead they won't have enough body left to tell I was even a guy.*

"Awake now?" said Stanis. Nicky could hear the smile on his face. It was the cold one, the one without teeth. Nicky managed a jerky nod, dragging his cheek across the burlap. He probably looked silly lying there like that, like a sack of mackerel, but he knew what he was doing. Even though he wasn't tied, he wanted to look as helpless as possible. He didn't want either of them to get the idea that he thought he was tough. *Fat fucking chance.*

"Good," said Stanis. "*Gregor's* idea is to kill you, now. *Gregor* thinks you are a liar. So. Are you? Are you a liar?"

Nicky did his best to shake his head but, lying there as he was, terrified to make anything like a sudden move, the best he got was a sort of shudder.

"Get him out," said Stanis.

Gregor's ugly shadow re-appeared, reached in and hauled him up and out. Nicky wasn't stupid enough to struggle.

•••

"Put him there," said Stanis.

It was the docks, the fucking docks. It was some warehouse that Stanis owned, or he owned the guy who owned it. Nobody was coming down this way until morning, at the earliest, if they came at all.

Nicky fought the urge to scream as well as the impulse claw at Gregor's massive neck and shoulders.

That guy was like a fucking Frankenstein monster anyway. Nothing outside a .357 was going to do anything but piss him off and, currently, the .357's were in short supply.

Gregor set him down on a cable wheel and shot him a look one might give to a disobedient puppy.

Sit, it seemed to say. *Or else.*

Nicky had seen *or else.* Stanis once let him watch Gregor play a song on Django Prokiroff's skull and bones for the better part of an hour. Django had shorted Stanis on some bookmaking scam or something (not Nicky's business) and Stanis wanted a message sent.

The message was, *If you fuck with my money, Gregor's going to kill you and take his sweet, Baltic time doing it.*

The irony of course was that Django never got the message himself. He was too busy getting murdered by Gregor to understand that he was an epistle. His slow gurgling death at Gregor's hands sort of cut off the info flow.

Everybody else, though, everybody unlucky enough to see what Gregor left of him, they got it.

Even the cops steered clear of Stanis after that. Whenever they did feel compelled to pay Stanis a visit, they always came six deep. Fucking punks.

Nicky didn't want to think about Django or the

cops. He'd never liked that little gypsy shit when he was alive.

Now that he was dead, and Nicky was about to join him, the last thing he wanted was Django's ugly mug floating around in his head. Nicky never liked to think about cops.

"Stanis," he started to say. If only he'd let him explain. If only he'd tell Gregor to take five so Nicky could make his case.

"Quiet," said Stanis softly. He meant it. Nicky had heard that tone before. His mouth snapped shut.

Gregor was rummaging around in the dark somewhere, pulling things down or apart. Nicky tried not to wonder what those things might be. Instead he watched Stanis watching him back. Or, rather, Nicky watched the patch of darkness that he knew Stanis occupied. He knew Stanis was surveying him with those milky undead eyes of his. That's what Stanis did: he watched. It was Gregor who did stuff.

There was precious little light in the warehouse, just what was coming through the row of small windows at the top of the far wall. Those were mostly covered in black paint. The rest was all wooden crates- stenciled with letters Nicky couldn't have read had there been light- and cardboard shipping boxes, miles of them. Nicky wondered for a moment how Gregor was navigating out there in the inky maze but then he remembered.

Gregor was a fucking monster. Monsters loved the dark.

A story from Nicky's school days, few and long ago, drifted through his mind. There was a fable or something about a killer with a bull's head who lived in some kind of tunnel somewhere. That was Gregor.

Stanis had told Nicky about Gregor once, where he'd come from: the *Stepnatz* or *Petsnits* or whatever. It was some Russian Death Squad thing. Stanis went on and on about how good they were at the wet stuff. That's what Stanis called breaking people's necks, cutting off their fingers, gutting them like fish: *The Wet Stuff.*

These *Petsnot* guys were supposed to have written the book. How Stanis got Gregor out of Russia, much less to the States, Nicky didn't know. He was here now, though, humming in the dark.

A table slid out at him from out of the shadows followed by a smiling Gregor. Smiling Gregor was infinitely worse than Scowling Gregor. A smiling Gregor was one that was or was about to be covered with somebody else's blood. The big Russian wrestled with the table, getting it into place.

What's next, thought Nicky. *Fucking tea service?*

Gregor leaned over him, close enough for the smell of that disgusting cologne of his to choke its way into Nicky's lungs. A light bulb, single and bare, clicked on above him and Gregor receded.

"Hands," he said as he went.

Nicky blinked at the shadows, uncomprehending. The sudden intrusion of light, even this tiny sphere of it, into the warehouse's pervasive dark was less than comforting.

Far from forcing the ominous shadows into retreat, the light threw the existing darkness into sharp and frightening relief. Now there were two worlds where there had been only one.

Gregor and Stanis were out there in the comforting

womb of black and Nicky was here, alone, in the light. If anything he felt more naked.

"Hands," said Gregor again from somewhere.

Again Nicky responded with blinks.

He was terrified to make any move, even one requested, in case his turned out to be the wrong interpretation.

Gregor circled around behind him, reached down, took the aforementioned hands and placed them, flat, on the table.

"No moving, liar," said Smiling Gregor.

No, sir. Not on your life.

"Now," said Stanis from the dark. "We talk."

"Sure," said Nicky, fighting a stutter. "Anything you want, Stanis, man."

"I want the truth, Nicky," said Stanis. "Simple, yes? The simple truth."

Nicky cleared his throat. This was it. Tell it, tell it straight or spend the night with Smiling Gregor.

"Okay," he began, looking for the right words. "Okay. It's like I told Gregor. I was holding the stuff, just like you told me. I even holed up at some piece-of-shit motel so's nobody would know where I was."

Gregor snorted, circling.

"You were alone there?" said Stanis.

"Yeah. Yeah. Of course," said Nicky. "I was just gonna, y'know, watch the cable 'til you called me. Shit, I gave Gregor the number."

No, he thought. Bad move. *Don't shift the blame. Stanis won't go for that. You did your best. Stanis has to think you did your best or it's over.*

"But," he went in again, more steady this time. "I got nervous. What if somebody saw me pick up the shit? What if they followed me, right, and they were just waiting to bust in and take it off me?"

"Yeah," said Smiling Gregor. "What if?"

"Hey. Everybody's got enemies, am I right," said Nicky. He was warming to the story, getting the rhythm. "Even you got enemies, Stanis. Somebody tries to take your shit off me, who'm I gonna call, right? Not you. Not the cops."

"Hands," said Smiling Gregor.

Nicky had moved them, using them to illustrate his points as he did when he was telling stories to people who weren't probably going to cut his intestines out. He set them back on the table where Gregor had put them.

"So," he began again. "I call this guy I know. Bruno. Him and me boosted a couple liquor stores back when we was juvies. When the cops finally nailed me I never gave him up. I figure he owes me."

"You figured that, huh?" said Smiling Gregor.

"Yeah. So he shows up and we're kicking it at the motel. Everything's peachy. But then he wants to see the shit. For himself, right? He wants to know how much is there, how much it's worth, all that."

"So you just show it to him, this Bruno?" said Stanis. The tip of his cigar was red hot. "You give him my heroin, my money."

Pull it out, Nicky, he thought. *Don't let it go this way. Don't let this dead-eyed bastard connect your dots.*

"No, Stanis, no. That's what I'm telling you," he said. "He just wants to get a taste, right. Just a taste. Keeps saying you're not gonna miss it. He's like spending the money while I'm sitting there. He's talking about all the cars he's gonna buy, the broads he's gonna screw."

"And you, Nicky," said Stanis. "What do you do?"

"I'm watching the clock, man," said Nicky. "I'm telling him to forget about it. It's stupid to even be talking about it."

Nicky took a pause then- a dramatic one, he hoped- and did his best to look appropriately stricken.

"That's when Bruno goes fucking postal on me."

"Postal," said Stanis. "What is this postal?"

Nicky explained postal.

Then he explained how Bruno's asswipe of a father was all the time giving him shit about how stupid he was, calling him 'shit-for-brains' all the time and 'fuckhead,' stuff like that.

He explained how, since then, Bruno went kind of psycho when somebody even got near calling him dumb.

The trouble was that Bruno's old man was right. The only thing quick about Bruno was his temper. The rest of him was about as sharp as bucket of mud.

"And so?" said Stanis, that hint of irritation creeping back into his tone. "What happens then?"

"He goes fucking psycho on me, man," said Nicky. "Like in-fucking-sane. Starts pounding on me, saying he's gonna kill me and like that. Then he takes the stuff and bounces."

There was a quiet and a stillness from the dark that Nicky was liking less and less. It was as if Stanis had somehow folded layers of the stuff around himself like a- what was the word- a veil.

As the seconds ticked, all Nicky could make out was that burning tip and the little tongues of smoke as they danced on the edge of the light. Then came the murmurs, in Russian, between his captors.

A tremor ran through him as he was assailed by thoughts of what specific little instructions Stanis might be giving to Gregor. He remembered how Gregor had started with Django's fingers. He remembered how Gregor was smiling.

"Stanis," he said, hoping he didn't sound as shit scared as he was. "It wasn't my fault, man. That's why I was coming to you instead of skipping; so's you could fix it. "

Something moved behind the veil, something that sounded like Stanis.

"I will fix it, Nikolai," said the Stanis-thing.

A shape arced out at him from the dark, a small red shape like a hockey puck, and skidded across the table.

Nicky stared at the thing as if it were an airplane and he was an aborigine discovering it on some primordial beach.

"Open it," said Stanis.

At first Nicky thought it was some kind of weird Russian joke.

Put your hand in the hole, see if something bites it off. Ha ha. Very funny.

Then he saw the seam. The puck was a box.

"Open it," said Stanis.

Nicky's hands twitched and inched, seemingly on their own, towards the plastic box.

He watched them as he might two rats fighting over restaurant leavings. They belonged to Stanis now.

The box popped open easily and the lid fell away. His hands were shaking visibly by then.

The tension was like an animal inside him, trying to claw its way out.

The box fell to the table, spilling its odd contents. Nicky puzzled over it for what seemed to him like hours. The thing was vaguely u-shaped; spongy, yet firm enough to hold its form when pressed.

Fuck, thought Nicky, realizing. *It's a mouth guard, a fucking boxer's mouth guard. What the hell is this for?*

"Put it in your mouth," said Stanis.

"My- my," Nicky tried but the word wouldn't come.

"Your mouth, liar," said Smiling Gregor.

"Put it in your mouth, Nikolai," said Stanis again, this time in that graveyard tone of his,

"But," said Nicky, stammering a little. "But, I mean, why?"

"Because I ask you to do it."

Oh, yeah. He's asking *me. He's* asking *his little buddy Nicky to just do him this in-fucking-sane favor because, you know, we're all friends here. Nobody's gonna get tortured to death for screwing up the simplest fucking job in the world, or anything. No way.*

Gingerly Nicky took the thing in his hand, felt the little weight it had, and put it in his mouth.

How'm I gonna talk like this, he thought. *I'll sound like a fucking moron.*

"I trusted you, Nikolai," said Stanis from the dark. "I let you in my business. I think you are quick, smart, strong. But you are weak, Nikolai. Weak."

Nicky began mumbling furiously but the plastic in his mouth made the words into little more than a

11

collection of simian grunts.

"No," said Stanis. "You are weak. To let someone take from you what is mine? No. You think this is a game we play? Games are for children, Nikolai. We are men."

Stanis emerged from the dark then, looking like a goddamn movie vampire. And, like the victims in those old black and whites, Nicky was transfixed.

He watched, rapt, as Stanis inched toward him, lingering over the intervening distance like it was the body of his favorite mistress.

Gregor, smiling, came after but stopped short of stepping fully into the light. Instead he just hovered there at the dark's termination point.

Stanis eased around the table's edge until he was standing right beside Nicky, until Nicky was nearly choked by the smell of pungent Russian cologne.

He sat on the tabletop close to Nicky's hands and looked down on him. He was still wearing that bemused half smile, the one that never meant anyone any good.

"Are you a man, Nikolai," he said softly.

Nicky managed a nod but was unable to produce even the slightest sound. He was the sparrow now, Stanis the snake. Everybody knew how that story ended. The only tension was in the placement of the strike. When? When would the teeth come down?

"Yes," said Stanis. "You think so?"

Again, with difficulty, Nicky managed a nod. He was sweating by then though he didn't know it.

"Well," the Russian went on. "A man understands pain, Nikolai. He knows pain like he knows his shadow. Like he will never know his wife or his children."

The cigar was done so Stanis crushed the butt dead– not on Nicky's face, thank Christ. He then reached lazily into his jacket, fishing, Nicky supposed, for the next tobacco spike.

"Gregor knows pain," said Stanis. "Don't you, Gregor?"

Smiling Gregor murmured something in Russian that made Stanis laugh. It was a sound Nicky hoped never to hear again in his life, however short that life proved to be.

"Gregor knows pain," he continued, still fishing for the elusive stogie. "And I know pain."

Nicky was really unhappy about the turn the conversation had taken. His forehead began to bead with sweat. His eyes began to well.

"Yes," said Stanis seeing the approximation of surprise cross over Nicky's face. "Oh yes, I know pain. But you, Nikolai, you do not know it so well, I think."

Stanis leaned in to Nicky, so close that the hair of his beard scratched Nicky's face as he whispered, "But I am your friend, Nikolai. I will teach you. I will teach you about pain."

Stanis was the watcher, Gregor the one with the dirty hands. That's how it worked. Stanis was old and smart. Gregor was neither but made up for it by being a total sadistic maniac, kept on a leash somehow by Stanis.

Nicky knew the leash was there. It was obvious. What the leash actually was though, he couldn't say.

So, even while Stanis was an inch from his ear, telling him some obscure Russian parable about friendship and pain, Nicky kept most of his attention on Gregor.

He never noticed the flash of the silver stiletto as Stanis whipped it from his jacket and plunged it into Nicky's hand.

He did notice the screaming though. Hard not to. He was the one doing it.

He didn't know how long it took him to stop or why Stanis slapped him every time he clawed at the knife with his good hand but, eventually, he did stop screaming.

"Good," said Stanis gently as Nicky moaned into the Formica. "This is my gift to you, Nikolai."

"Pissed himself, I bet," said Gregor. He wasn't smiling anymore. He looked disappointed somehow.

"No, Gregor," said Stanis. "Nicky is a man now. He understands my gift. Don't you, Nicky?"

From somewhere in his painful stupor Nicky dredged up a final pathetic but visible nod.

"You see," said the Russian. He sounded cheery, like he as strolling through Chastaine Park chatting about some cute kid playing fetch with a puppy.

He stood, clapped Nicky on the back as if to say, *Good Boy. Nice work*, and wandered off into the dark. With a dismissive grunt, Gregor followed.

Nicky listened as the staccato of their footfalls dwindled to almost nothing. When he was sure he couldn't hear them anymore he reached for the knife and braced himself for the pain of withdrawal. It took him a second to work up the nerve.

As his fingers tightened on the knife's handle he heard Stanis' voice again, like a whisper, but from everywhere at once.

14

"Tomorrow night, Nicky" said the voice. "Tomorrow night you will return to me what is mine. You and this Bruno. You will do this or I will give you another gift. One closer to the heart."

"I won't say I'm not disappointed. I'm not a moralist. This works fine in Las Vegas, in Reno, in Amsterdam. Somehow those cities have managed to have legalized prostitution, for decades now, and the wrath of God hasn't come burning down from the sky. But you know what has happened? Those cities have increased revenue, the women in question have healthcare, stability, safety, are free from drug use-well, as free as the rest of the population. Maybe it was a political mistake to push so hard for this; we'll see in November. But this city is dying and if we don't employ some out-of-the-box thinking to save it, it's going to take a lot of us with it."–Councilman Gerard Woodman, MORNINGSTAR PRINT NEWS, September 15, 2010

TRACK 2: GLOOMY SUNDAY

The *Mercy Motel* was about as close to hell as Layla ever hoped to get– fifteen dank, sweaty rooms, two temperamental soda machines and no ice.

The manager, a rolly bowl of lard named Halo something, ran hookers out of any rooms that were unoccupied, which was most of them mostly. She could hear them on occasion, *"ooh-ing"* and *"oh baby-ing"* for the twenty-dollar Johnny Tricks who came to the Downs for the premium blend of fantasy and squalor that only Halo's pros could provide.

She'd found the Johnnies pathetic at first, just busters too stupid to see through the pancake and spandex to the disease factories beneath.

She had sympathy for them because they were so obviously out of their depth.

After a week of listening she revised her opinion. The pros were the victims if anybody was. First of the Johnnies who thought less of them, really, than the condoms they occasionally agreed to use.

Then, worse than the Johnnies to her mind, the pros were the victims of Halo who took most of their earnings- hard fucking earnings- and handed out beatings and put-downs in return.

Yeah. She felt sorry for them, but only from a distance.

She'd seen what life on the stroll had done to her mother, after all. She knew the bargains the pros made to make that life bearable.

"I got that good shit for you, baby," Halo had said on her first night and every subsequent time their paths crossed. He was a gelatinous man with his name in gold across his top front teeth and a diamond in the hole of the O. "Anything you want, any time you want, come on down to Halo."

Yeah, right, she'd thought. *Sure, I'll do that. Right after I chug down this bottle of rat poison I keep handy.*

Yeah. She knew the bargain. She knew it wasn't one.

It would take more than anything ten Halos had to turn her out. Anyway, she had her own thing going with Nicky. This thing he was running was going to net them enough chips to cash in and fade the hell out of the Harbor for good. That's what Nicky said, anyway.

Nicky, Nicky, Nicky, she thought in a sort of nonsense singsong. *Nicky, my love.*

Well. Maybe not *love* but close, as close as she was getting. She'd outgrown the pink angora sort of sentiment in her teens and hadn't looked back. No more Whoever and Layla, sitting in Whatever trees.

Nicky had his faults *(oh yeah, deep dish buckets of faults in that one)* but he made the bells ring when he was of a mind. How many guys could say that?

Why else would little Layla put up with the schemes and the overnight absences and the occasional back of the hand? Why else would she be sitting here in the dark, watching pay-per-view porno, waiting?

Silicone Chick One, the blonde, was blowing the police commissioner while the chief and his wife,

Silicone Chick Two, were lubing up his secretary for a threesome.

Been and done, she thought, stifling a yawn.

Even the performers looked bored with the whole thing.

Anyway, the last aspirin was wearing off. Her eye was beginning to hurt.

The bruise, bigger now and purpler, looked even worse under the bathroom's harsh flourescents. It throbbed there on her face like some kind of weird mutated organ.

The Thing from Planet Eggplant, she thought and smiled.

The make-up wasn't coming close to hiding it. Nicky did a pretty good tune up when he got going.

This whole thing with Stanis and the drugs had him riding a wicked harsh edge.

She should have known it was going to come out somewhere. She should have known not to dump any extra on him. He had his limits and, when he passed them, that left hooked out at whomever was nearest and smallest.

Mostly, lately, that was Layla.

They'd talked it through like fifty times, of course. Nicky was big on *plans* and *getting over*.

Layla thought he used the yack-yack to get himself charged up. Sometimes it was even fun to watch his hands flying around his head when he was deep into describing some new scheme or some pearl Stanis had dropped.

Other times, lately, the talking only made things worse. Nicky was climbing the rungs, sure, but he was also getting on Stanis' nerves a lot more too.

Stanis was not somebody you wanted mad at you. Hell, Stanis wasn't somebody you wanted aware of you, if you were smart. Layla made sure she stayed well clear.

Nicky thought he could dance that Mafia dance, though. He thought he could get cozy with them, make some real money for a change. And it seemed like they thought so too. Stanis was giving him real stuff to do finally, stuff that mattered.

So, where was he?

Stanis liked him. Stanis thought he was a good bet. Stanis had called him over for some quick meeting about Mafia things like two hours ago.

So, where was he?

"Don't worry, babe," he'd said, patting her ass. "This is gonna be cake. Just keep it running 'til I get back."

Keep it running. Right. That's what those boring-ass pornos were supposed to be for– Nicky's idea of foreplay.

He'd lit out of there, amped for his meeting, with visions of her doing her best Kim Basinger or Ava Gardner for him on his return. He should have come back quick and with three fucking legs.

So, where was he?

A halfhearted squeal from one of the porno chicks pulled her out of her head. She wasn't a natural worrier, not little Layla.

Her own mother had called her *Frosty the Snow Bitch* when she was only ten. She could get a handle on something as simple as his tardiness, right? Right.

•••

Okay. He was late. Really late.

So, maybe, the meeting went long. The Ivans could stretch a drink out for weeks if they were of a mind. Maybe they were at some Black Sea strip joint, bouncing nickels off Ninotchka's ass.

Maybe he was twitching in a gutter somewhere, bleeding to death.

"Oh. Yeah," said one of the porno chicks, or both of them. *"Fuck me."*

Layla shut the medicine chest and, just for a second, caught her reflection in the mirror.

"No," she said to it. "Fuck me."

•••

A lot of people who work in restaurants or diners will tell you they're not superstitious. They see too much of the ass end of human behavior to believe for a second in anything remotely like magic.

There's no magic in some jerk that thinks his Rolex or his Beamer is a license to leave his prints on your ass.

There's no magic in a coke-snorting boss that gives bonuses to the girls who can make his blood flow south. There's no magic in mopping up somebody else's puke at the end of a twelve-hour shift.

A lot of people who work in restaurants or diners will say that all they believe in is the clock and the tip. If they do allow a superstition it is this: some waiters, some of the time, get a sort of tell when something bad is going to happen on their shift.

It'll be something like a queasy stomach or a suddenly twitching eyelid that will alert them that tonight might have been the night to switch with the new girl.

"I knew it," said Frances as soon as Layla walked

into the diner. "I *fecking* well *knew* it. "

Frances claimed to be a British import of some kind but she never could get the accent quite right. She got pissy when anybody quizzed her on it or on her hometown or on why the cops over there didn't have guns or how the hell she'd ended up in the Harbor.

She was full of answers too, though none of them matched. Her history was as malleable as her accent.

Nobody much minded. She was one of those busty, cookie dough girls- a little bit crunchy at first but, with the right kind of chewing, pliable and sweet.

Layla couldn't remember where they'd met- bouncing at some club or on one of Nicky's marathon dive bar binges- but they kept running into each other for a while and now they were calling themselves friends.

"Hey, Frances," said Layla pulling up to the counter. "How's life?"

"Better, now that Graham and the Brat have fecked off."

Frances always said *feck* instead of fuck. It was one of her things. Another was updating Layla on the ongoing soap opera of Graham and the Brat.

Graham, it seemed, was a low-end lawyer and wannabe hood who had a thing for girls in plaid skirts and blazers.

He'd been cute once, back before the Flood, but now he was well into his seedy decline. He dressed up, okay– suit, shined shoes and a fat wallet– but there was a pallor to him, a sallow caste to his skin, a greasiness to his hair, which made a person think of dead smelt.

So far, appearances to the contrary

notwithstanding, his quest for jailbait hadn't dipped below the legal age of consent. According to Frances, the Brat was pushing it, though.

"Eighteen if she's a day," said Frances more than once. "Don't care what that license says. Mine says I'm twenty-two."

The Brat was a skinny, sway-backed little sports coupe with hair out of at least two bottles if the combo of burgundy and brunette was any clue. She wore the buttons of her white school shirt mostly *un*.

Ditto, the buttons on her blazer. The navy blue tie was just a strip of cloth around her bare neck, hinting so much of a leash and collar that it made Frances sick to think of it.

Everything the Brat did or said or wore was for effect, everything. She was a gum-popping, man-eating, bundle of sex and she knew it. Hell, she worked it.

She was sure working Graham.

He'd stuck with the Brat for almost six months now, a record for him.

Frances thought it was because, despite her youth, the Brat had found just the right balance of pout and fondle to keep Graham's attention on his crotch instead of his wallet. Graham spent, the Brat collected and, occasionally, they gave Frances a show.

Tonight's update had them fighting about Graham's wife and what he was going to do about her.

Graham said he wasn't planning on doing anything about her. What would he do?

The Brat had ideas; they started with divorce and ended with a smash on the head followed by a quick trip to the morgue.

Graham wasn't having any. He was married, staying that way and, if the Brat had a problem, she could find some other pony to ride.

The Brat, feeling that half a year on his arm entitled her to just a little more consideration, handed Graham an ultimatum. Either he gave the wife her walking papers or he could mutter his late night confessions less horizontally and to someone else.

That earned the Brat a slap that started the screaming and brought the two burly Puerto Rican cooks from the kitchen to haul the both of them out.

At the end of it all there was food everywhere but, surprise, no money. Worst of all, Frances had been running a fever all day; her tell for the inevitable bad shift. She should have known.

"Wow," said Layla at the end of this. "So, have you seen Nicky tonight?"

"Nah," said Frances. "And maybe you don't need to either. You know: considering."

She meant the shiner. Layla had thought it nicely hidden behind her oversized shades but, apparently, it was not. She shifted some of her hair to hide the edges of her face.

Tonight she was a redhead; Nicky liked redheads.

"Should tell that berk to piss the feck off," said Frances.

"Should floss my *fecking* teeth, too," said Layla sharply. "He been in here tonight or not?"

Frances shook her head. "I'm well serious, Layla," she said. "You don't wanna let that tosser bounce you around like that much longer. One night you won't bounce back."

"Christ, Frances," said Layla. "Don't start that shit,

now. Okay? I ain't in the mood."

"I'm just saying–"

"Yeah, well, save it."

"You can do better, that's all."

"I'm doing fine," said Layla. "Drop it. "

"But how many times are you gonna let this fecker–"

"You got a customer," said Layla, thankful for the reprieve. Frances was a decent chick and all but she had no *fecking* clue what she was talking about.

The two women looked the newcomer over as he stood, dripping, by the far door. It hadn't been raining when Layla walked over from the *Mercy*. Or maybe it had and she hadn't noticed. At any rate it was coming down now. The guy was soaked.

"Just grab a menu and take a seat, okay, luv?" said Frances, flashing her best May-I-Help-You grin. "I'll be right with you."

The dripping man nodded politely, scooped up the big duffel he had with him, and drifted towards an empty booth at the far end of the diner. Layla watched him from behind her Ray Bans. Even partially blocked as he was by Frances, there was plenty to see.

He was a big piece of masonry, wasn't he? Not linebacker material, maybe, but not somebody you wanted to be on the wrong side of either.

He had balls of steel too, to be on this end of the Downs, on his own, at night. Black guys didn't last too long below Bender Avenue, even in daylight.

The Ivans and the few leftover Goombas didn't take too well to the monkeys coming over the wall.

Well, if he didn't know the rules yet, he'd better hope his first lesson wasn't his last. If he did know the rules and was here anyway, he might bear watching.

"And you, little miss," said Frances in a conspiratorial murmur. "You are fecked in the head."

"Your date's waiting," said Layla, gesturing towards the big man.

"Bitch," said Frances.

Layla blew Frances a kiss and moved to a booth where she could watch both the door and the street with ease.

It was raining out there, hard. The sheets were thick enough to smudge the other buildings into little more than a collection of immense geometric shapes; an artist's impression of a city.

On any other night Layla would have welcomed a cleansing shower. Anything that left the streets of the Harbor unsoiled and blew the smog away for a while was okay in her book.

But tonight, when she might have to go out into that soup to find Nicky, when he might be lying, shot or stabbed, right across the street and her unable to see it for all this wet? Not okay. Not okay at all.

She would have to do something, though, and soon if he didn't make an appearance somewhere. Maybe she should have stayed at the *Mercy* after all. It was where he would expect her to be, where he'd told her to stay. Maybe.

It was hard sometimes explaining to him why she hadn't followed some instruction of his to the letter. It was hard for Nicky to grasp that sometimes things came up. Sometimes you had to detour or cool your heels or find some other way to get whatever it was you were doing done.

Yeah. She should get her ass back to the *Mercy* and

wait by the phone. If he hadn't checked in by morning– well– it would be morning. If he hadn't turned up by then she'd know he wasn't going to.

"What's with the wig," said a voice behind her.

She'd glanced away from the door for a second to take another look at the street. The voice drew her back and she saw him standing there, just standing there, like he wasn't three and a half fucking hours overdue.

"Nicky!" Then she was all over him- kissing, fondling, telling him how worried she'd been.

The barrage went on for a second or two until she settled into hanging comfortably from his neck.

She registered the odd way he was holding his arms, how he wasn't wrapping them around her.

"Yeah, yeah," he said, shrugging her roughly away. "What's with the fucking wig?"

"You like red," she said, crestfallen. "You said–"

"Whatever," said Nicky.

He winced as he dropped down onto the booth's torn vinyl and Layla thought she saw some kind of dark stain on his shirt.

Nicky, once he was settled, ignored both it and Layla. Instead he turned and yelled for Frances to "get her fat ass" over to him.

Layla, buffeted between the joy of seeing him alive and apprehension over this new dark mood he presented, slowly lowered herself into the opposite side of the booth.

She watched, stifling a gasp, as he placed his hand on the counter. At least she assumed it was his hand. Everything below the wrist was a mass of torn cloth and dried blood.

"Jesus Christ," she said when she'd processed what she was seeing. "What happened to you?"

"What the fuck do you think?" he said. His fingers, the good ones, were tapping against the Formica table top like hailstones. "The fucking Ivans showed up early."

It wasn't hard pulling the story out of him. Nicky always wanted to talk. It was both the best and worst thing about him.

The plan had been to take the bags of smack and cash and pretend that Nicky's idiot friend Bruno had lifted them.

The Ivans would find Nicky "unconscious" in the motel room and he'd put them on Bruno's trail.

They'd find Bruno but, by then, the money, Nicky, the drugs and Layla would have faded off to someplace sunny.

Layla pictured him standing there in the little room trying to decide on the most dramatic pose for Stanis to find him in.

Only, after Nicky had taken delivery, after he'd handed Bruno the duffles with his future in them for safe-keeping, Bruno had disappeared, leaving Nicky to watch the clock and wait for Stanis. But it wasn't Stanis who showed up, was it? No. It was that human slaughterhouse, Gregor. And early on top of it.

After a beating– Gregor gave those out like candy– the Russian dragged Nicky to see Stanis.

"What did you do?" she said, incredulous.

Her visions of Nicky twitching to death in some rain filled gutter had not been far off target. That he was sitting here telling her anything was far less likely. Yet here he was.

"What do you think I did?" he said, a hint of his normal bravado returning. "I ran the scam. So the timetable was off. So what? These fucking mooks ain't brain surgeons."

"Did they go for it?"

"What the fuck do you think?" he said, raising his wounded hand. "Why do you think he did this?"

Layla blanched again at the sight of his blood and the gaping hole in his palm. This was the Ivan's idea of letting him off with a warning.

"He wants his money, okay," Nicky went on. "He wants his money and his smack back or he's gonna smoke me and anybody who was with me."

He went on after that with details of his torture and how he'd cleverly talked his way out of a dirt nap but all she could here were the words and anybody who was with me echoing around her head.

"You didn't tell them about me, did you?" she finally managed.

"Why the fuck would I tell him about you?" said Nicky as he swiveled his head I irritation. "What do you have to do with anything?"

She hated when he was like this, all belligerent and defensive and taking shit out on her. She hated it but she was used to it. She knew better than to keep pressing.

Annoying Nicky when he was like this was like dropping a bottle of nitro into a volcano.

It occurred to her that he really was like that when he went boom; like a goddamn hurricane, a force of nature.

Her best bet now was to hunker down and hope the storm passed soon.

"Well, now, let's see… basically, for every year you sign up you get ten thousand bucks on top of your pay as a solider. That's 10k for one year, 20 for two, 30 for three and, yep, you guessed it, for a four-year commitment, we give you a 40k signing bonus. That's standard. But let's say you got a skill the army needs, like, something with computers or you're a fantastic mechanic or you know Arabic or Farsi, then we tack on another 6k per. Yes, that's firm, in your hand, cash money. We're fighting two wars, son. Two at the same time. It ain't like the old days when the government would just grab the guys they need, run 'em through Boot and put them in country. Nope. This is the all volunteer army now. Every man and woman in there wants to be there. Tell the truth, if it was up to me, I'd check out and re-up just to score some of this loot. Yeah, I'd back up my old pick-up fill the bed and sing Yankee frikkin Doodle all the way to the bank." **Army Recruiter, November 18, 2009 - MEDGAR EVERS HIGH SCHOOL, GRAY HARBO**

TRACK 3: MECCA & THE SOUL BROTHER

Max hated the rain. It made everything gray and slippery and hard to hold onto. You couldn't get a real grip on anything when it came down like this, not even directions.

Then again Fall, in Gray Harbor, was never kind. The air was *always* a little too damp, the clouds *just a little* too close to the black side of silver.

There was *always* something predatory about the way the wind kicked the refuse up the alleys or swept between the legs of the unwary, something sneaky.

It was as if the city knew a harsh time was coming and it just couldn't wait.

Even in this light drizzle edges blurred together, colors bled into each other and the kind of telltale noises that gave you warning if somebody was creeping up behind or lurking in some up-ahead doorway got beat down to nothing by the *tackattatackattatackatta* of the drops.

Even if all that wasn't true, there was the hell of just getting around in all that wet.

This current storm made just getting from the bus station to the Downs on foot into the kind of forced march you might hear a preacher read about Moses or Noah doing back in the day.

People like that were always climbing mountains or fighting monsters or living through some wicked bad disaster. They had God backing them up.

Aside from his duffel and the Pea Coat keeping

him warm, all Max had to fight the rain was the
Marine-issue poncho he'd copped from the PX.

Jesus, he thought, looking around at his old haunts,
seeing them altered by years and choppy memory.
Turn my back for a second and look what happens.

Even without all that gray dripping all over
everything it was easy to see the kind of damage six
years could do to a place.

Big Willy's Joint was closed and gone, with Big
Willy probably the same. The sign was still up,
hanging lopsided off one rusted length of chain, but
the store underneath was empty.

The place wasn't just closed down but boarded up
and plastered with ads for some local rap crew and a
50's Do Wop reunion show. It was like somebody had
tried to erase *Big Willy's* from the neighborhood but
got bored with the job halfway through.

Max remembered spending hours slapping a
baseball into that sign while he hung with his crew
after practice.

Even with all the boards and rotting paper all over
everything, he still half expected Willy himself to roll
out, hollering about how the reason he couldn't get no
foot traffic was 'cause of all these damn street
hoodlums lounging on his corner.

"I ain't no hoodlum," Max would say.

To which Willy was expected to come back with
something like "Shit, nigga. Could of fooled me."

Max hadn't known it then, and even if he had
would never have admitted it, but he sort of loved that
big old tub of South Georgia guts.

The Side Street Arcade had turned itself into some
kind of twisted mix of a recycling drop and a launder-

o-mat that almost put a smile on Max's face.

Just the idea that the place he and Lavall had dumped so many quarters and wasted so much time had figured a way to take both from people without providing any fun at all was somehow funny.

Lots of the houses were boarded up or burnt-out or boarded and burnt.

He'd seen a news story about the Devil's Night festivities a couple years back. Apparently nobody had cleaned up since.

Hell, if anything, they'd added insult to the injury–graffiti tags now covered almost every visible surface like syphilis scars.

What a trip.

Getting himself out of the Downs in the first place had been a fucking miracle. Coming back and finding it like this? He wasn't even sure there was a word for that.

Stranger than the fact that half of the places he remembered were gone or changed was all the signs in Spanish and Russian that were up all over.

Yeah. The neighborhood had changed all right. Even the *Q Spot* had morphed into one of those *24-Hour Breakfast Houses* that seemed to have sprouted up every twenty miles on the interstate.

"Eggs over-easy with sausage," said the chubby blonde, thumping the hot plate of food down in front of him.

She made the retro pink uniform bulge in strange places when she moved. He wouldn't have thought so before seeing it but Max found the effect strangely enticing.

"Be right back with the pancakes."

She was a foreigner of some kind– you could tell by the accent– but he couldn't place the actual country. Not that he ever sat still long enough in the Triangle to tell a Brit from a German or whatever.

He gave her a nod and got down to business on the food. It was still coming down hard outside so there was no reason to rush the meal.

One thing you could say about these 24-Hour joints, they were always toasty as hell.

Anyway, he still hadn't exactly worked out his game plan.

He had numbers to call. Martine was nice enough to front him those after a long lecture about keeping his black ass out of the Downs if he knew what was good for him. Wasn't growing up there enough? Hadn't he burnt all his bridges getting out the first time?

Yeah. He had. Everything she said was right– but there were other issues.

"Still a damned fool, huh, Max," she'd said. "Don't you know there ain't nobody in the world as lucky as you need to be."

"Yeah," he told her. "But still."

And then she gave up the numbers she had, all four of them.

Martine. God damn.

Just thinking about her took some of the chill off him. She was always on his list back then, why not? Even at fourteen she had a body to make a guy break his neck for a look and it only got better every year after. Not that she gave a shit. All she cared about was putting the Downs behind her.

She was one of those hard-to-peg sisters– hot like

fire, nose always in the books, but ready to scrap if things turned that way.

Just about every yo in the neighborhood had tried to climb Mount Martine one time or another but not one of them even got to set up a base camp.

"Think I'm letting one of you little ghetto niggas punk me?" she would say. "Shee-it. Second I graduate I'm so ghost it ain't even funny."

She wasn't lying either. The ink wasn't even dry on her diploma before she was up and gone. Max had been shocked when she took time out from her fast getaway to give him her number in NYC– just in case.

"You ain't like these other busters," she told him as he walked her to the train station. "You got a head. You ever decide to use it, you can call me."

He had no clue what she was talking about, which seemed to both disgust and amuse her. She pressed the number into his hand and disappeared into the rest of her life.

Martine was just one of those people whose head Max could never get in.

You ran into them once in awhile– folks who didn't jump left or right the way they should and never gave up the reason why.

She grew up two blocks from him but she might as well have been from the Moon. He always regretted never getting in her pants.

"–the fuck you talking about," said the guy in the booth across the aisle.

For a second Max thought the guy was talking to him but, when he looked up, it was instantly clear that he was still dogging the chick he was with.

Max had pegged their whole story the second he'd

set eyes on them.

Didn't matter that they weren't the expected neighborhood color; the guy was a hitter and the chick would spend her whole time with him with her back on the ropes, waiting for somebody to throw in the towel.

She'd either get wise, jump off in the next couple years, or she wouldn't and the train would run her over.

The younger Max would've walked over and checked the loudmouthed bastard, thrown a scare into him so he'd shut up at least.

The older Max knew better.

Punking out some guy in sight of his chick was bad enough. Checking Mr. Wifebeater in front of his favorite punching bag could get the girl killed.

Still, it was no fun to listen to.

"Look, just shut up," said Mr. Wifebeater.

"I just want to know what we're gonna–?" said the girl.

"There ain't no 'we,' okay," he said, slamming a hand down on the table, rattling the salt and pepper shakers. "There's just me and the fucking migraine you're giving me."

Max didn't know if the chick was stupid or just hungry for a smack but, the madder Mr. Wifebeater got, the more she kept coming back at him.

She was smart enough not to come at him too hard, at least. It something she'd probably learned from the back of his hand.

Dodge, weave. Give him some gas and maybe you'll get what you want.

It was a good push as far as it went. She never got

near to really challenging him in any way, just kept pressing whatever it was she wanted to know.

Still, it was a risky little jig she was dancing, stupid even. Anybody could see this guy was two or three fuck-yous away from an Assault and Battery jacket.

Well. Almost anybody.

"I'm just saying," said the girl. "This whole thing's fucked. You get in any worse than you are, you're gonna need an undertaker. We gotta think about–"

There was another smack of flesh against formica and then the conversation went quiet again.

In spite of his irritation at the whole display, Max was interested in the mysterious subject of their discussion. He shot a quick glance their way, just to see if the girl was still holding her own.

She seemed to be, barely, sort of.

They were huddled in the corner again, not cozy but close and conspiratorial, like they'd just remembered a secret they wanted to keep.

The girl was sort of nestled up under the guy's arm now, making soft noises of agreement with whatever it was he was saying.

She was okay looking for a white chick– not hyper skinny, not too chunky. Max always went for the ones with a little meat on them. That anorexic, fashion mag shit was for punks.

Her hair was that color red only rock stars and hookers ever seemed to bother with– maybe just a wig, once he looked close.

Her jacket was a heavy leather thing– probably lifted from a previous rider– that looked like it had been dragged behind a pickup for a hundred miles.

Ditto the military style steel-tip boots and faded

black jeans. He was surprised to see that she actually had a little muscle on her. Maybe she wasn't just a punching bag after all.

Looking at her on her own you'd never think she'd be the type to fall for this twitchy car wreck of a guy. Hell, his bloody hand should have been the stop sign at the end of that street but, from the look on her face, you could tell the girl didn't see it.

He had the hook in her deep and he wasn't about to let go until she stopped twitching. Max had seen it before and, if he stuck around long enough, he was sure he would see it again.

The 'hood made a lot of chicks like that– willing to latch on to the first strong arm that flexed in front of them, even if the arm smacked them around a little. Shit, some of them even got off on the hard knocks. Made them feel like they mattered to the guy or something. Stupid.

Well. It was her life to toss. Maybe she'd have better luck on the flip.

He was just rounding up another forkful of runny eggs when he felt the wifebeater's eyes on him.

Say something, he thought, watching the guy through the corner of his eye. *I dare you to say one motherfucking thing.* But the guy didn't. He just dredged up a smirk and went back to mumbling with his chick.

Max lifted out the word, Bruno from the rest of their muttering and what sounded like monkey but that was all. Before he could figure out if the monkey was meant for him, his waitress returned with the pancakes.

"Hey, Francie" said the guy as she set down the

plate. "Get your fat ass over here. I need a drink."

Francie flushed, clearly a little embarrassed by the language or maybe just that Nicky-guy's presence.

She flashed Max an apologetic little half-smile, turned and said, "Sod off, Nicky. You see I'm working here."

They exchanged a couple more jibes– obviously the other two were more than just random customers– and then she disappeared into the kitchen somewhere.

The rest was pretty uneventful. Max chewed and swallowed and the Hard Knock Couple kept mostly quiet.

When Francie came back with a coffee refill, he asked her about the local motels– the *Mercy,* the *Waterfront*– and whether either of them was still in business.

She'd never heard of the *Waterfront* but the *Mercy* was still up and running. The place was a shit-hole if his memory was right but he'd only need it for a couple of nights.

After that, one way or another, he'd be taking Martine's advice.

"I think the simplest way to answer that is this: In our research we've determined– that is, the data seem to show– whatever the economic circumstance, whatever the level of available technology, whatever the era or the region of the world, human beings tend to cluster in groupings, numbers, that can be held in the mind easily. The city, as useful as it is on a macro scale, is largely an abstract concept when one tries to picture it in the mind. What people can hold, the largest grouping, is Tribe. That's a network of extended families, essentially, and we see it played out in city after city in neighborhood after neighborhood but, and this is interesting, these tribes are not connected via bonds of blood. The old bonds of genetic family have broken down largely in favor of this sense of, I suppose, urban tribe. We think there's something powerful there but, as yet, we're not sure if it bodes well for us, as a species or if it bodes ill. We need more time to examine the data." – **Dr. Anissa Gruenwald – from TED DIDN'T TALK TO ME - ESSAYS & INTERVIEWS FROM THE REAL CUTTING EDGE, (published 2015 by BATTERSEA BOOKS LLC)**

TRACK 4: MERCY STREET

The *Mercy's* black and white contours loomed over them like the carcass of a giant killer whale, beached on the concrete shore of the street that shared its name.

Layla took in the sagging retro-deco awnings and the faux wood shutters, all painted in a version of blue that had to be seen to be nauseated by.

Halo's lights were on and the shades closed, indicating that he was busy setting up a trick for one of his girls or testing the merchandise himself for quality control.

The lights flickering on the drapes of numbers four, nine and twelve said that most of the ponies were running so he was probably bringing in some new talent.

Though the picture of some barely-out-of-her-teens chippy on her knees in front of that evil tub of guts wasn't one she liked to have in her head, it was a damn sight better than Halo himself leaning out and making his standard leering advance.

Home again, home again, she thought as she tried to help Nicky out of the cab and along the narrow walkway that led to their room.

He kept shrugging her off, grumbling that the last thing he wanted was her hands on him right then. He had to think, damn it, and he couldn't to it with her pawing at him.

She'd thought the trip to the ER and the subsequent

juicing with painkillers (not to mention getting the hole in his hand patched) would have improved his mood but, if anything, he had sunk even further down.

He hadn't even come out of his funk to give her shit for wasting money on the cab or on the Bullet Bags they'd got at the Gangbuster Grill's take-out window.

He was down at the bottom of his head somewhere in that place Layla knew better than to disturb him.

"Keys," he said with his hand out. She handed them over, mindful to keep quiet and a couple steps back while he wrestled with the door.

He set them up in the last room at the rear corner, the only one whose door faced the back fence. His idea was that it was the most privacy they could get for the money and, since you could hear anybody approaching on the walkway, they couldn't get surprised there either.

Layla had thought it was a damned easy place to get stuck with no way out, a murder scene waiting to happen, but she'd been wise enough to keep that to herself.

Nicky only had a couple of uses for chicks and advice wasn't on the list.

"Well?" he said, shoving the door open and lurching inside. "You wanna stay out there and drown or what?"

•••

The sex was crap. He just climbed on, pounded away for a while and then, when he'd got his flash, climbed off and went back to brooding.

It wasn't like she'd been into it herself. It was just, after the night he'd already had, she figured it was the least she could do. She did have a selfish motive. For Nicky, a good bounce could blow out the cobwebs and improve his mood. Mostly that's how she kept the peace between them. Not tonight though.

Tonight all she proved was that Stanis could stab the life out of anything, even a fuck.

She pulled all the blankets together around her and folded herself into a horizontal ball, the better to watch him sulk. Normally she'd have washed off the whole evening with a quick shower but then she'd never seen him in this dark of a mood.

Not that he didn't have good reason. If there's one thing folks in the Downs had learned since the Ivans moved in it was that they didn't joke around about murdering you. Usually they didn't even talk about it. You just crossed the line and woke up in a box or, more likely, in ten boxes, in twenty pieces at the bottom of five storm drains.

He already looked a little like a corpse, sitting there naked under the single yellow bulb. The light hanging over his head made dark hollows of his eyes and cheeks and threw his ribcage into uncomfortable relief.

When did he get so skinny? she thought.

•••

"Thing is," he said, after a dreary silence. "This could still work if I could find that gump, Bruno."

His confusion was understandable. Nicky had known Bruno for a long time. If the guy managed one coherent thought a month it was cause for fireworks and beer. He was big, thick, deadly as a tire iron to the skull and more likely to set himself on fire than jump once Nicky told him to stay put.

49

And yet there was no answer at any of the numbers Nicky had on him and no lights in the window of the room at *The Waterfront* Nicky had told him to take.

"You think he really did skip out on us?" said Layla.

Nicky didn't know what to think but he wasn't telling her that. Bruno was a God damn moron. No way he had enough brains in that monster skull of his for a double-cross. But there was also no way he wouldn't do exactly whatever Nicky told him right down to the letter.

Nicky had put in too much time on training the big mutt. The idea that he had enough push in him to make his own plans was just a joke and not a good one.

Something was up. Something had put a snag in this and Bruno was hung up in it somehow.

Fucking Bruno, he thought. *Goddamn, fucking Bruno.*

It wasn't enough he had to juggle all these fucking angles, on the fly. Now he had to come up with a way past all this that didn't end with him hanging on a meat hook somewhere watching his life making a red puddle beneath him on the floor.

•••

Click!

The *Mercy* was exactly the shit-hole he remembered, now complete with resident pimp, hooker stable and the assembly line of guys whose wives or girlfriends just wouldn't bend they way they wanted. Or maybe they were just sick twists who had to pay to get their particular kind of sweaty. Most likely that and nothing Max wanted to think about in any case.

The rain had trickled out on the long walk from the diner and, after he was out of a quick cold shower and into some clean new gear, he was hot to get going. He hadn't missed the Harbor while he was away and didn't want to spend one second longer than he had to back in its crumbling guts. This was a straight bag and tag mission- his version of one anyway. *Get in. Do the recon. Identify and locate the target. Execute. Simple.*

Except it wasn't. Because all of Martine's damned numbers were dudding out on him and whoever that was next door seemed to think the best way not to get their face smacked in was to keep up that slow rhythmic *boom-boom-boom* on their side of the wall. Max was about two seconds from going over there to show them how bad that idea actually was but, first, he had his own business to sort.

None of Martine's numbers worked. Either they were just DOA or they connected to voices that weren't happy to hear Max's. He knew that would be a problem, considering how he'd left things when he'd left, so he'd been making the calls on a burner phone. No sense giving some of these people a way to track him down after spending so much time disappearing.

Anyway. He still had a couple to try before he had to fall back to Plan B (whatever that was). He scanned the first set of digits that didn't have a thick black marker line through the center and dialed.

"Yeah, who this?"

"Max, Smokey," he said. "Trying to get hold of–"

"Wait, hold up," said the voice, obviously tensing. He could actually hear the grit coming into Smokey's voice like gravel filling a trench. "Max? Max

Pilgrim?"

"Yeah, Smoke," he said. "Look, we ain't got to get into no old shit here. Just trying to-"

"Nigga, you must be tripping," said Smokey, his voice turning from gravel to burning coal. "You must be out your damn mind, trying to hit me up for anything."

Smokey went into a tirade composed of barely comprehensible *"fuck you's," "nigga's,"* and *"bitch made punk's"* before settling into something between a growl and a mutter.

"Reggie, Smoke," said Max, trying to keep his own pressure down. Smokey was a crackhead little twitch the last time he'd laid eyes on him, a spindly slip of a guy who nobody who liked breathing would turn their back on but he had one redeeming quality that Max needed to get at. "Just trying to put a number next to Reggie. Last I heard ya'll two was still tight."

The phone went click before he got to finish. Well. Smokey had a right to be carrying the torch all this time. Max had done him ill, after all. At least from Smokey's POV.

He drew a line through the number and moved on to the next.

Forty-three seconds later:

"God damn it, Vernice!" he was standing on the bed, growling into the phone because he didn't want to scream. She had no reason at all to be acting this way. She barely knew him. All she had to do was give up a number. "This ain't nothing to do with you and all that old shit! You know where Reggie's at! Just give me the God damn–"

Click!

"Fuck!" he said, to no one in particular. "Fuck, fuck, fuck!"

The phone went flying before he could stop himself, ricocheting off the closet door and back into the moldy bathroom where, he could tell from the very final sounding crunch, he was going to have to pick up another burner before going on with this.

Thing was, he still wanted to hit something. It was a big chance he took coming back to the Harbor and, the longer he stayed, the bigger it got. Having to put up with even two seconds of shit from these half-pipe hood rats just got him boiling again the old way.

But, of course, it was the old way that had put him in this mess to begin with. It was the old way that had set him running out of the Harbor in the dead of night and forced him to sign up to go shoot at one set of angry men with guns in order to escape another. The old way was the thing he had spent eight years putting down and he wasn't going to let these low-end scrubs make him pick it up again.

He made his breath slow down to something like normal. He sat heavy on the ancient, brittle sheets, letting himself be lulled by the familiar rusty creak of the bedsprings as they bent to accept his weight.

"One more number," he told himself. "It'll be the one." Then he could track down Reggie and all this shit would be done. Yeah. Perfect.

He retrieved the burner, happy to find it not quite as thrashed from its impact with the moldy porcelain as he'd thought. It lit up fine when he flipped it open and there was a tone when he hit the buttons. Good. Good.

He was just getting set to dial when something

thudded against the wall, hard, and the woman next door started screaming.

Although the problem is frequently overlooked or denied, anyone can be a victim of domestic violence, regardless of age, size, or gender. Being alert to the warning signs of domestic violence is the first step to ending it. No one should live in fear of the person they love. If you recognize yourself or someone you know in the following warning signs don't hesitate to reach out. Help is available. – **PUBLIC SERVICE SIGNAGE on a bus stop at the corner of Hearst and Simpson, Gray Harbor, USA on Sept. 17, 2009**

Or the bitch could just shut the hell up–
anonymously spray- painted across the bottom.

TRACK 5: VOICES CARRY (ACOUSTIC)

"Nicky?'

"Just shut it, Layla," he said, not looking up. "Can't think with you clucking in my goddamn ear."

"I'm trying to help," she moved close to him, her hands running soft up his back, across his shoulders. "If we talk it out maybe we can-" The back of his hand caught her hard across the cheek and sent her crashing into the headboard, which, in turn, smacked hard against the wall.

The world split into two distinct visions- one a grainy black- and-white like an old *Twilight Zone– (The Terror of the Girl in the Box)–* and the other was a blood red and ink black snapshot of the seedy motel room with Nicky swirling around the center like Satan or somebody.

As her brain fought to bring the two images back together she noticed distantly that he was on his feet, his scarecrow fingers fiddling with his belt.

She watched him, groggy from the swarm of bees that was suddenly inside her skull. The buckle, one of those rodeo knockoffs depicting a horse and rider in assembly line relief, was wider than necessary and made of something other than the steel it counterfeited.

Steel or not, she'd felt that buckle before and ached for days after from the marks it had left.

"Baby," her words were still slurry. The bees refused to vacate. "Honey, no. What did I do?"

"Always, talking," he said through his teeth. The belt and its buckle went up and down, smashing across any part of her she couldn't cover with her hands. "Always got something to *say.*"

"Baby, Please. Stop."

"I told you to shut it," he said, the words coming staccato between the blows, accenting them. "I told you. I told you. I fucking told you."

Every syllable was punctuated with a strike and she could tell, even through the pain and the buzzing swarm in her head, that he was just getting warmed up.

She tried to send herself away to that cold quiet place she kept inside- the little room in her mind that life with her mother had built- but she couldn't find the door. And even if she found it, she would need the key, the concentration to block out the pain and the screaming of the lunatic she was saddled with.

This is your own fault you stupid shit, she told herself.

She knew better than to press Nicky on the best of his bad days and this was the worst. She knew better but she had to know, didn't she? She had to know what the Ivans knew.

The thought of Stanis, dead- eyed and stinking of foreign smoke, rolling her name round his mouth like a hard candy before he gave it to Gregor was too terrifying to let sit.

They were nightmare people now, living in the silence between the strikes of the belt and the haze of buzzing creatures in her mind.

A vampire and a zombie shooting craps for the privilege of first bite. And Nicky was somehow the chef, their Igor, tenderizing her for them with the buckle that went up and down, up and down across her flesh like an iron fist.

Layla heard her voice, still begging for him to stop, but it was like she was on auto-pilot, hanging between her body and the hope of safety from her secret room. Even if she couldn't quite get there, the hope of it protected her from some of the pain. Some was better than none. She wasn't even counting the blows anymore. After twenty, what was the point?

"You listening?" his voice came from some place even farther away, somewhere unimportant. "You gonna start listening?"

"Yeah," she wanted to say even though her mouth would only beg. *"I hear everything you say. I know everything about you. I know what you are. Who else could ride the Nicky Train like me? Who else can take this shit?"*

She wanted to say that and a lot more but she would have to go back into her body for that and that just wasn't happening. And, anyway, something had just crashed open their front door.

She heard the sound, a hard short thunder crack in the universe off to the left and felt her eyes swivel slightly in that direction. A hulking black shape hung in the open rectangle for a second, maybe taking the sight of her in, maybe deciding if it wanted to play too.

For a horrible moment, less than a moment really but it seemed like forever, she thought it might be Gregor come to teach Nicky the right way to beat his girlfriend to death. It wasn't.

When the figure stepped inside the light from the

59

overturned lamp showed him to be that black guy from the diner. He was dark jeans and a grey tee and hard black boots and he was moving for Nicky like a machine made for murder. There was something cold in the black guy's eyes that she recognized and welcomed.

"What the fuck?" said Nicky just before one of the massive brown hands took hold of his wrist and the other wrapped itself around his throat.

He gurgled something that sounded like the beginning of a threat before the bigger man spun his body around and slammed his face into the floor right beside Layla.

She swore she heard something crack on the impact and wondered if it was something inside Nicky or the floor.

"Miss?"

Layla heard the word, or thought she heard it. Somewhere on the other side of the door to the little safe room she kept in her head, someone was talking to someone. All she'd needed was that one tiny break in the storm of belt buckle and she managed to open the door and slip herself inside.

It was quiet in there. Safe. She could think. Make plans. She could live in the space of that little room the way she never could in the world.

Her books were there where she'd left them, all two of them. The copy of *The Story of O* she'd swiped from her mom she wished she could throw away (yet never could) was perfectly pristine, its cover uncreased and still sporting that weird glossy shine.

The other, *The Prince,* was so over-read it looked like something you'd find in a pirate's tomb.

The little Stickly end table, with its draping of grannie's lace shawl, still sat by the windows. The sheer cotton curtains, closed of course, but still letting in that inkling of sunlight, twisted a little in that very slight breeze that was always present here but which she could never feel.

The bed, that overstuffed iron-framed thing she'd had for six months when she lived with Jumper in Arcadia, was still there, would always be. Unmade, its sheets and blankets an off-white swirl of beckoning comfort, reminded her that, for those six months at least, she had really been a teenaged girl and she had really been in love.

She'd tried to bring Jumper himself into the room more than once but, for some reason, he wouldn't come. He was good for sex fantasies and for beating herself up with when she thought about how she was with Nicky but, for this room, no. This was a different kind of safe than he could give her, even as a memory.

"Miss," said the voice again, low and growly but not threatening somehow. It reminded her of a cartoon show she'd seen where a boy and a bear had adventures on the Mississippi river.

Hello, Mr. Bear. Why Hello there, Billy.

"Miss, you okay?"

For now she was, safe in her room, but she knew, if the voice kept on, it would pull her out again. It was harder and harder to get here and, once inside, she had to be careful not to leave too early or stay too long.

Too early and whatever it was she had run in to hide from might still be out there, menacing. To long and she might not ever leave and that would mean she really was crazy after all.

61

Only she wasn't crazy. She was safe. This quiet space was the place where she could sit and think after all and, no matter what anybody else out there thought, Layla liked to think about things. She thought about herself, about her evil twist of a mother, about Jumper's golden skin and hair and their dreams of following the surf and the surfers from beach to beach forever.

She thought about the plans she had for the future- yeah she had plans, her own Layla plans that ended with her and her man in, well a nice house and room just like this one only real- She thought about everything in that room. Everything.

"Miss," said the voice, calm but insistent. "You need a doctor? You want the cops?"

No. No. No cops.

Something about cops seemed very wrong for right now. Not just because of the room, the sweet bright safe room, but because cops would make things outside harder to navigate.

There'd be statements and lawyers and some fat oily bitch telling her how she was a victim and how she needed to get out of the spiral she was in before it was too late. And at the edge of it all, the zombie and the vampire waiting for her blood.

"No," she heard a voice like hers say, soft and far away. "No cops."

The door opened and through it she could see the other room, the real room, the one she shared with Nicky at the *Mercy*.

The big black guy was there, bent over a pretzel thing that turned out to be Nicky. The guy's knee was in his back, one hand on his head, pressing it down.

The other hand held Nicky's arm up, out and back, twisted very much wrong and was probably the cause of the anguished look on his face.

"What the fuck," he said straining to get a look at the attacker. "Who the fuck are you, man?"

The black guy- Jesus, he was like a wall of bricks- told Nicky to shut it. Then, "You sure?"

"Yeah," she knew it was her voice. It just seemed so far off. "Yeah, sure."

The open door grew wider and wider until it and the *Mercy* had swallowed her safe white room. She was back in her body again.

"Look, what the hell," said Nicky, trying stupidly to struggle and groaning when the black guy gave his arm a sharp twist. "You ain't no cop. You got no idea what-" Another sharp twist and grinding of muscle and bone put the message finally into his brain.

The black guy looked up, his dark mahogany eyes boring into her. That cold thing she saw before was in there again, like miles and miles of glacier ice.

"There's two ways this can go," he said softly, almost like he was talking to a kid. "I can make it so you never use this arm again or you can say you're sorry and take a walk."

It took both of them a second to realize he was still talking to Nicky and, when they did, Nicky surprised her by managing a croaky little laugh.

"Who are you? Mr. Rogers?" he said, wheezing from the pressure on his back. "I ain't sorry for sh-!" The rest was a scream from the black guy yanking back on Nicky's arm and, it seemed to Layla at least, putting even more of his weight into his knees. "Okay. Okay. I'm sorry. Shit. I'm sorry."

"Okay?" said the black guy, never taking his eyes off Layla. "That good enough for you?"

She felt herself nodding. Yes. Whatever. This was crazy, anyway. Who did this guy think he was?

She watched numbly as the black guy hauled Nicky up to his feet and marched him out the front door. As soon as they crossed the threshold he shoved Nicky out into the rain soaked parking lot and waited. The second Nicky was on his feet and sure the black guy wasn't going to shoot him or something he started screaming.

"You are dead, man. You are so fucking dead! You got no idea who you're fucking with!"

The black guy took a step, one step towards him and Nicky let out a little *eep!* and scampered, actually scampered off into the night. Wow.

She drifted a little, her mind wandering into whiteness and thoughts of Jumper and Bruno and the Ivans and-

"Hey," the black guy was crouched in front of her. His tone was still soft, even a little concerned, maybe, but his face was like stone. "You probably want to put on some gear and get ghost. Your boy was shook up but he's coming back. You know this, right?"

She felt herself nod.

"So?" he said.

"Look," she managed after a little time figuring how to work her lips again. "I'm cool. Okay. Don't worry about it."

"That's a mistake."

"Whatever," she said and, realizing suddenly that he could see the blue star tattooed over her left nipple, groped around for a sheet. "I said it's cool."

He made some weird noise in his throat, like a hum or a cough, that didn't quite make it and then reached around behind her.

The white sheet floated over her like a shroud, gravity pulling it down her body until her face was exposed again. She looked up in time to see the front door closing behind him. She was alone.

It took her ten minutes to let that single tear fall.

RESPONSIBILITY TO PROTECT: The responsibility to protect is a set of principles based on the position that sovereignty is a responsibility, not a privilege. Under this paradigm, states must focus on preventing and halting genocide, war crimes, crimes against humanity and ethnic cleansing. If the State is unable to protect its population, the world's other nations are responsible to help the State do so.

If a State is manifestly failing to protect its citizens from mass atrocities and peaceful measures are not working, the international community has the responsibility to intervene, at first, diplomatically, then more coercively, and, as a last resort, with military force. - From Webisaurus, a free internet encyclopedia

TRACK 6: LAY LOW (CLEAN VERSION)

He lay on the bed, staring up at the cracks, wondering. His list of pros had dipped pretty low while his cons just kept stacking

Martine's numbers were bust, all of them. He was sitting on just under five hundred bucks and about two days before the wrong people figured out he was back in the Harbor. He had to execute or abort and get out before then or- well, he'd seen *or* in the desert.

Or left its head in the rubble a rocket attack had pounded it and the old family hovel into. *Or* spent the last ten minutes of its twelve short years twitching and coughing in a lake of its own blood. *Or* went out hard and ugly because it didn't keep its mind on what was what.

He wasn't going out like that if he could help it.

So, tick tock, Max, he thought. *Figure this shit out.*

The thing was, as he riffled through the names and places he had in his head that connected in some way to Reggie, he kept getting pulled up short by the face of the girl next door.

It wasn't like she was familiar to him or anything, certainly not from the old days. There was just something about that face.

It wasn't the eyes; he knew that. They weren't any special shade of blue. Hell, they were as faded as old denim if it came to that. It sure wasn't the streetwalker red she had in her hair like a neon ad for escort service. It wasn't her bloody lower lip, probably still fat from the belt buckle dance.

No. It was none of that. But it was something.

He thought he could hear her, shuffling around next door, maybe still in that one white sheet or maybe, finally, in some clothes and on her way out. He swore he heard the door open and shut at least once and maybe her talking to somebody in a low nervous voice but he could have been dreaming it.

He could have been pasting on his own ideas for her too. It wouldn't be the first time, would it? It sure wasn't the first time he'd stepped in where he wasn't asked and done at least as much harm as good.

Learning that lesson was turning into the hardest thing of his life. If tonight was any proof he still hadn't quite got it. The sound of that girl squealing, begging, getting pounded like that, it was, well, he still hadn't learned that lesson. Maybe he never would.

He caught himself listening again in spite of himself for the sound of her, listening and not thinking about his own business, and then he thought, *Got it.*

The Downs was different now, sure, with the names all in new languages and the new faces all so pale but there was still that old slaughterhouse stink all over everything.

A year of rain wouldn't wash that away and, just like all those old faces and places he remembered, the girl had that same stink on her, that same caul.

She might as well have had *I'm never getting out of here* tattooed on her forehead just like the blue star on her tit. He'd seen it a million times.

Didn't matter she was white or that she was probably going to be dead inside a month from this current guy or some new more perfect copy. All that mattered was that face kept him from thinking, which was what he needed to do.

There was something weird there, something besides the bruises and the fear and that tweaky faraway place he watched her come back from.

One second she was all empty and headspun like a broken dog and the next she was back in there telling him everything was cool.

He'd seen crazy before. Shit, he'd been crazy, to hear some people tell it, but he'd never ever seen a switch like that. Trippy.

No, he scolded himself. *To hell with that chick. She's nothing to you. Get your head back on business.*

Nobody who knew him wanted to know him anymore and he shouldn't be surprised. He never expected Reggie to be easy to find.

The phone wasn't going to work so that meant he had to get his boots muddy and he couldn't waste time doing it. There had to be somebody left who didn't want him dead.

He just had to figure it. He just had to

The fire was everywhere, faster than expected and spreading in ways he couldn't have thought. There were footsteps and screaming and he had to get out too before the place came down around him. He had to get out but he wasn't done looking.

In the dream he was never done. He ran, screaming a name- sometimes Reggie's, sometimes Captain Wallace's, sometimes his own. Shit, it was a dream, so it didn't bother him to be looking for himself sometimes. Everybody did that. The fire was the point. The fire and the looking and the not finding before it was too−

He was awake again before he realized he'd drifted off. He hated the damned dream but he loved how it cleared the deadwood. All those phantoms just burned away in the flames leaving behind the thing he wanted. He didn't have any friends here anymore and he didn't have numbers or a place for Reggie but now he had something that was better. He had a name.

Lavall.

The name was electric, salvation. Lavall would know. Lavall knew everything. No matter how many Balkan death squads moved into the Harbor you couldn't get Lavall out without mortars and satchel charges. Hell, even with that. Lavall. Lavall would know.

Max just had to get there.

•••

He was up before the sun as usual so he got to see the cold fingers of light tripping slowly over from the east. First there were the black shadows, darker even than the ones the moon cast on those nights when the clouds parted enough to let it show through.

Then there were the silvery halos that seemed to erupt from the corners of the distant skyscrapers, imbuing them with a spit-and- polish quality that, just for a second, gave you a sense that the Harbor wasn't a hungry, rabid, dying beast.

Looking at it in those first moments of day you could kid yourself that there was hope out there and maybe, just maybe such a thing as luck.

At least that's how Max felt looking at the light spilling out over the brick and stone and steel. Maybe this shit would all work out after all.

He felt that for the entire ten minutes it took for the sun to crest the city's edge and then he got down to business.

He was a Harbor kid. He knew the rules.

You don't get anything out of the place that you don't cut out yourself and maybe not even then.

He knew it wasn't likely, even if he did track Reggie down, that the rest of it was a crap shoot at best.

He'd skated the odds once, barely. It was possible he could do it again. If not Max, then who, right?

As he locked up his moldy little room at the *Mercy* he felt the steel returning to his spine and the necessary frostiness returning to his mind.

He had to be a machine today, talking no shorts or excuses. Lavall would be full of both and he didn't have time to navigate all the normal twists and turns.

"Hey," said a voice, drawing him out of his head. He turned to see the girl from last night hanging in the doorway of her room.

She looked a little better. She was dressed, if you could call it that, in the sheet he'd left her in, now wrapped around her like a toga.

The red hair was gone, obviously just wig, and the close cut blond reality gave her a pixieish quality that he almost liked.

"Hey," he said. He slowed to be polite but didn't stop walking.

"Early start, huh?" she said. "Getting a jump on stuff?"

"Yeah," he said, sort of turning her way. "You could say."

"So," she said, letting it trail. There was something

in her tone, something like, *Hey. Stick around for a sec. Let's talk. Let's have a coffee or a scone or...* But he didn't have time for *Or,* whatever that meant to her. He was on Lavall and then Reggie and that's all.

"Look," she said, firm and retreating at once. Nice trick. "Just hold it a second. I want to-"

She was beside him, suddenly; the sheet, sticking on the asphalt, drew out behind her like a bridal train.

Her hand went to his shoulder.

She didn't actually touch him but the gesture was enough to stop him and get him turning her way. It was also enough to yank half of her home made toga down across her chest, exposing her little blue star.

Max was careful to keep his eyes on hers. She looked all soft and half pounded but she could be just as much a viper as anybody else in the Harbor. Even the kittens had teeth.

"What," he said, giving nothing and taking nothing from her.

"Nothing," she said peering up with those giant blue saucers. "I just wanted to say- y'know- just- *thanks.* For last night."

"Easy," he said. "Don't worry about it."

"No, it's," she made a show of finding the words, maybe real, maybe winding him up for something. "I feel like I owe you something, right."

"Like what?" he said, wondering how long it would take her to hide her blue star.

The longer it showed, the less he trusted what she said.

Chicks didn't make mistakes like that or, if they did, they fixed them fast and did a little dance of embarrassment to make sure nobody got the wrong notion.

This one wasn't dancing.

"I don't know," she said. "I just feel like I owe you some-"

"You don't," he said, doing the I-really-should-go thing with his shoulders. "We're square."

"We're not," she said. "I owe. You know I do. So I need to pay you back."

"We're square," he said again. "It wasn't personal, okay. Could have been anybody."

She laughed at that, a strangely musical little thing that was sort of out of place coming from her. Like a ten-year-old wearing all her mother's make-up at once.

"It wasn't anybody," she said. "It was you."

"Yeah," he said. "It was me. And I say we're square, okay. Now, I gotta go."

He didn't wait for an answer and he didn't look back but he was sure the star was still out.

It didn't matter. Nothing mattered except Lavall and, through him, Reggie.

Find Lavall. Make him talk. Move on to the next. That was the drill today.

Only the local transport wasn't holding up its end. Lavall would be holed up somewhere in the C Section, up in those housing projects he treated like his personal kingdom.

That meant a trip across the Downs, over hundred blocks of what had become dark territory in his time away.

Navigating all the neighborhood borders and local customs was hard enough when he'd been in the mix himself. Jumping between Harp Street and Best Way was like hopping the fence between Artashat and

Igdir. Worse. Now it would be suicide. Harder in its own way than getting around the desert.

So a quick march wasn't the way to get there and that meant cabs or busses. A cab would cut into his funds too much so that meant strap hanging for the twenty or so minutes it would take to get across.

Only there was no bus. A little under an hour later there still wasn't.

"Well, hey, again," she said, cruising to a stop beside him. It was the girl from next door again, now driving something that had probably once been a car, probably a Japanese import of some kind, but only back in some distant time before the Flood.

Since then the thing had obviously been to the bottom of at least one sewer, been kicked around by something wearing work boots the size of a St. Bernard and had survived a firefight if the bullet holes under the left rear window were any hint. It had been red once, maybe, that bright tomato red that the yuppies all liked for about a year.

Or maybe that was just the remnant of leftover rust. Now it was mostly primer, duct tape and a bumper sticker across the front of the hood that read SUCK IT, HATERS.

"Hey" he said, not really looking her way.

"So..." she dangled the word on the edge of what was quickly turning into a smile. "You're waiting for the bus?"

He nodded. Of course he was.

"Yeah, that's gonna be awhile."

"How's that?" he said.

"You missed Devil's Night," she said, the grin actually showing now. It spread across the bottom of her face like a Playboy centerfold lounging in a Tahitian hammock. "Didn't ya?"

Of course he had. He'd missed eight Devil's Nights in a row and eight Christmases and eight New Year's Eves. He'd missed the whole Harbor and everything in it. That's what running away meant: running the hell away.

The "so what?" must have shown on his face because she broke the smile long enough to answer it.

"I wasn't here but the Ivans all say the *herps* went ape shit on D Night about two years back," she said. "Some kid got popped by the cops 'cause they thought he was robbing a store. Turns out he was just making deliveries. They shot him like thirty-nine times or something. Ten-year-old boy. Cops got off. So... BOOM!"

He didn't ask her what *herps* meant. It was the same word in every language. Even the desert people had a version.

"'Boom?'" he said.

"Boom and a half," she said, leaning back to savor the image. "They said it was like Judgment Day around here. Shops burning, guns going off every two minutes. People getting tossed out of windows. And that's just the stuff they got on the news. You sure you don't know this?"

He shook his head. This tidbit of local history had escaped him in his travels but he knew his city. Every few years there was a riot over something. Taxes were too high. Cops didn't treat the blacks as good as the whites. Schools were all fucked up. Somebody got beat down when they shouldn't have. Somebody didn't who should've.

77

There was always something to get hot about in Gray Harbor and always somebody willing to put a brick to a skull over it. That was just how the Harbor was.

Maybe that was what happened to Big Willy and the other missing familiar faces. They got burned out or shoved out by their friends and neighbors.

"Well," she said, lost in her story. She was telling it just to tell it at this point, he thought. Him being there was just a bonus. She liked to listen to herself. "Thing is, about three hours into it, this bus driver tries to make a stop. White guy, right. They said he'd been running the same rout for like twenty years. Guess he figured he was safe or something. He wasn't.

They stopped the bus. Like a hundred people just laid hands on it, right. And they started shaking it. Rocking it back and forth, y'know. And this guy's trapped inside.

I can see him like screaming for help or whatever, like telling them he was their old buddy or something or like just trying to finish his route. Do his job. Something. But nobody was listening that night, right. He was just another white guy to them.

They turned the bus over right there in the street. They dragged him out and they just, like, started raining bricks and trash and whatever else down on him. Killed him. Right there, in the street, in front of like a thousand people they went like Full Biblical on this guy."

"They ever catch who did it?" said Max, knowing the answer.

"You kidding?" she said with a snort. "Turns out, even though there was a thousand people down there, at least, everybody was looking the other way."

Yeah. That figured too. That much *fuck you!* squeezed down into one place and you're going to have some shit pop off.

Then after, when everybody's back to normal, nobody saw a damn thing. Nobody would want to be reminded of what they turned into in the dark.

Sure. He knew that story. He didn't need to be there.

"So, anyway," she said, perking up and facing him again from her side of the open window. "Bottom line is the city don't run any buses down here no more. No buses, barely any cabs. Just the two subway stops and whatever else you can scare up."

Damn it. God Damn it! This was just the perfect twist on a shitty day and it wasn't even noon yet. *Shit!*

"But, you know, I got nothing on my plate right now..." Again the words seemed to hang on her smile just a second longer than normal before diving off. "I could probably take you where you want to go."

•••

Probably the first thing she'd learned when she realized she was capable of learning was that people usually do one of two things: what they can get away with and what they can't get around.

The big black guy definitely had the look of being in the second class, which suited her just peachy fine. People against the wall were easy to predict.

"So," she said, once he'd settled in beside her. "Where to, Boss?"

The C Section as it turned out. Awesome.

Not the first place on her list of happy fun locales and not the seventieth either.

The Ivans were one thing; they were thick and drunk as often as not and as sadistic as a team of Nazi prison camp docs but they followed rules. Once you knew where the lines were it was easy enough to color inside.

The C Section was, well, for the melanin-challenged it was like the Downs was for the blacks. A pale chick could maybe, if she was hot enough and kept moving and talked a good game, maybe walk through to the other side provided the sun was up.

Thing was, Layla wasn't on her game just now and, even when she was, she wasn't dumb enough to cut across the Section for no good reason.

Still, she needed Big Black to stick with her for as long as she could hold him so...

"C Section it is," she said and gunned the engine.

•••

He didn't say much over the first six blocks, just stared out the window, clocking the landmarks, lost somewhere in his head. By block ten the quiet was kicking her ass so she filled it up.

"Layla," she said. When he didn't answer or even glance her way, she said it again.

"What's that?"

"My name," she said. "You know: like the song? Clapton? Shit, my mom was like a fiend for him, y'know? Better than what she was gonna go with first. Didi. Yikes, right? I mean, what's that? Didi. Sounds like a little cartoon bird or something."

He looked at her then, straight on, scanning her the way he had back at the *Mercy*.

Tick Click Rattle Click.

She felt she should actually see the gears in his

head working. *Is this chick real? What the hell kind of name is Layla? What the hell does she want to do me a favor for?* All that was percolating in his head and probably more.

She gave him the *and you?* look and waited at the next red light.

"So, you got a name," she said when the waiting got old. "Or should I call my Psychic Friend and ask her?"

"Max," he said, eventually.

"'Max' huh?" she said. "Well, don't hurt yourself squeezing out a whole sentence or anything." He just looked at her and the light went back to red. "Max what?"

"Just Max," he said in a way that told her that was all she was going to get.

"Maximillion? Maxwell? Maxfield?"

"Just Max."

Jesus. This guy was a fucking vault. She joked around with him a bit more, yacking it up about his quiet ways and dropping her mother's theory about Still Waters on him to see if she could get a rise.

"Mom always said still waters don't run anywhere. They're just, y'know, still," she said as they passed the third Bullet Burger joint in as many blocks.

The traffic had actually gotten thicker as the moved off from the Downs. The streets had more people on them too. The buildings were the same dilapidated wannabe bomb craters but, somehow, at least for the moment, there was life out there.

"Still waters are still 'cause there ain't nothing going on under the surface," she said.

Nothing.

The words just seemed to fall into him like one of those black holes the PBS people were always going on about. Like an empty bottomless vacuum.

"So what do you think about that," she said, pressing. There had to be some way to pull the trigger on this guy's chat box. "That sound like you at all?"

"Yeah, sure," he said as if he was discussing the value of two identical grains of beach sand. "That's me."

Yeah. Right, She thought. *And the star on my ass is blue.*

She reached for the radio, praying that today was one of the days it would be sweet and actually tune in on an actual channel. If this guy was going to be the Black Lagoon, she was damned well going to have somebody talking.

If there was one thing Layla hated it was empty space and silence. If things were too quiet for too long her brain started ticking and that was never ever a good thing.

Figures the radio had to choose today to be a little piss pot. No matter how or which way she turned the cracked plastic knob, all she produced was varying degrees of static.

After exhausting all the FM possibilities several times over, she bit the bullet and flipped over to AM. The static there was like a billion fingernails running down a billion chalkboards, setting her molars on edge.

She gave up the ghost, flashed Max a wan little grin– *sorry for the shit condition of the ride, homeboy-* and hit the brakes. Red light.

The seconds of silence stretched out between them.

Her fingers drumming on the steering wheel sounded like a distant earthquake. What the hell was up with this guy? If she couldn't see his chest rise and fall and the occasional blink of his eyes, he might as well have been a corpse. Freaky.

She fidgeted with the coin box and the broken lighter and that weird compartment under the armrest whose name she didn't know and, finally, even dusted off the old adjust-the-rear-view-mirror for no reason trick.

"Shit," she said in a voice like the hiss of a dying radiator. "Shit a fucking dick."

Something in her tone got Big Black's attention because he roused himself from whatever dreamland he'd been wandering and looked as if he might speak. he never got the chance because, before he could push out a syllable she had floored the accelerator.

The little Japanese engine revved fast and hard as the car lurched forward, against the red light and into the metal river of cross traffic. Big Black cursed as she swerved to avoid an oncoming pick-up and was slammed into the passenger door but she paid no mind.

Threading in and out of the vestiges of the morning rush, she cut her little ancient car a path that clearly had her passenger thinking she' had lost her mind.

"Shit," she muttered, glancing into the rear view whenever she could safely spare the look. "Shit, shit, shit, shit, shit."

A hard right on Clemens, a harrowing rush down the access alley behind the *Super J Market* followed by a pigeon-dispersing bolt across Hargreaves Circle and the car finally came to a stop in the lee of the industrial-sized dumpster that had conveniently presented.

Layla slumped against the wheel as if she'd been shoved, her knuckles as white as bone because she couldn't relax her grip.

"Jesus!" said Big Black. "Jesus Christ, what the fuck is wrong with you!?"

Finally, she noted with a little dark spark of glee. *At least that proves the guy is human.*

"Sorry," she said, at last between the gasps. "Sorry. I just- I thought I saw Nicky back there."

She could see the *"Who the fuck is Nicky?"* on his face but his mind obviously supplied the answer before he could ask.

"Oh," he said. "Mr. Wifebeater. From last night."

She managed a nod. Forcing the hyperventilating to stop was proving tougher than expected.

"You saw him?" he aid, looking out the back window. She nodded again. "What on the street?"

"Car," she said. Her breath was regular again. She took her hands off the wheel and flexed them to get the blood back in. "I think we slipped him."

"You kidding?" said Big Black. *Max.* His name was Max. "You could'a killed us."

"Could'a, should'a," she said. "I said I was sorry. I panicked, okay? Shit."

"Yeah," he said, instead of whatever else it was he had planned before he saw how totally freaked out she really was. "Okay. Just relax for a sec. Take a breath. Chill. It's done, right? Everything's cool."

She closed her eyes and leaned back against her seat, making a small show of calming her self for his benefit. She still needed him after all and she didn't want him thinking she was too nuts to stick with. Not yet. Especially not now.

"Where the hell did he get a car?" she said, more to herself than anything. Max flexed his shoulders almost imperceptibly; his idea of a shrug. "Prolly boosted it. Stupid fuck. He's already got two strikes. Idiot."

She went on talking to herself that way, calming herself further by talking herself through a litany of his stupidities and shortcomings. It actually helped. Even Max seemed to finally shift back form what could only be described as Alert Status to what was, apparently, his default mode.

"So we're safe," she said, putting it to rest. "Otherwise he'd be here now. Already."

Max, apparently satisfied that her assessment was correct, didn't respond to that other than to settle back into his seat and resume staring out through the windshield.

Yummy, she thought. *Back to the silent treatment.*

•••

Once upon a time, way back in the 1960s, the blacks pretty much ran Gray Harbor all the way from Checker Square to the water. It wasn't that they liked it that way.

The Old Downs had once been called Niggertown because the rat infested, roach ridden acres of shanty and slum were the only places decent folk would allow them to set up when they migrated in from the South.

Niggertown was originally only about fifteen square blocks back around Depression time and just after the big War. But, like a lot of middle-sized cities, the Harbor got a huge bonus of negroes starting in

1953 or so and continuing up until the Actor got the big White Chair in DC.

Somebody needed to work the mills and factories and the white guys wanted a lot more money for that than the black ones would gladly take after their thrilling time under Jim Crow.

It was a win-win on paper but, of course, paper and life had little to do with each other.

They might have had a name for it in the South, a good old friendly name like Jim, but in the North and the Mid West and the West and pretty much everywhere, folks were less homey.

Naming the thing meant admitting it was a thing and things had to be dealt with. Things required opinions and opinions required decisions and decisions made waves so, no Jim Crow outside the south.

Only, of course, there was.

Like a lot of cities that had their own versions, Gray Harbor tried to ignore Niggertown as much as possible. There was an imaginary line running from the west end of Wallace boulevard to the corner where it intersected with the north-south running Loop Road. On the southeast side you were in the real Gray Harbor, the one with the shops and the street cars and the libraries and the Mayor.

On the Northeast side and all the way to the water: another country.

People crossed over, inevitably.

For the folks who lived in N- Town it was mostly for work. For the people who called it Niggertown the crossing was mostly for booze, music and that dark sort of adventure that some white Harbor kids learned to dream about listening in secret to their parents' lurid tales of the goings on "up there."

Mostly the two worlds kept their distance. In its heyday N-town had its own movie houses, its own markets, its own dance halls, its own schools- such as they were- and even its own doctors and lawyers.

The feeling there seemed to be, "Hey. Screw 'em. They don't want to let us in except to mop their floors? Fine. We'll do our own thing."

And they did. They lived in the real Harbor's shadow for decades, its darker sibling, its vibrant, musical, angry reflection.

But things, as they do, happened. King got killed. The Kennedy boys too. X. That mess in South East Asia kicked up. A president finally got caught doing dirt. Finally, the last straw some might say, the Actor took over the White House. Crack took over the streets. Eventually Ivans and Latins came in from wherever and the mills and the factories moved out.

All there really was left was the docks and warehouses and the Ivans took over most of that pretty quick. They weren't too keen on the *herps* and they let everybody know with beatings and bullets until the Downs was much smaller and the C Section was all the herps had left.

Max knew some of this. He'd grown up in the Harbor, after all, and a lot of it was street legend. As they left the downs behind and crossed over into the Section he ticked off the places he knew and the events that made their fame.

Corner of Market and Stone: Flick Johnson shot Lew Reitz over the affections of a dancer called Chantilly Rose.

The hooked street lamp that hung over Carson's Bakery: Little Perce Washington got hung there because he'd whistled at Phillip Enwright's daughter Jewel.

The New Public Works Building: rebuilt on the ashes of the old because one Byron Banneker had set fire to the old when he felt just one too many kids in is neighborhood had died from rat- bite fever.

Banneker was always Max's favorite.

When they asked him for his last words before they dropped the noose over his head, Banneker just said, "Y'all rather do me like this than help them kids. And you call me a murderer."

That stuck with Max when he learned it, though he couldn't exactly say why. Something about that proud sad man standing there waiting to die and still giving those frosty-eyed bastards the needle made Max proud. Layla knew none of the Harbor's long story and didn't need to.

A city was a city and the shit that happened in a city was just what happened. You surfed the tide or it crushed you– end of story.

In any case, the upshot of all that history, known or unknown, was that the blacks were only in charge of one part of the Harbor now: the C Section. The current rulers of the place were the Blue Dogs. Another foreign import, this time from the West. The Dogs came in with the crack and never left.

The Ivans had the Downs. The Dogs had the Section and Layla's little car had just crossed the border.

"Now what?" said Layla.

"Colmer street," he said.

"Fuck," she said. "Not the towers."
"Yeah," said Max. "The towers."

"Stop here," he told her and she was grateful. She hadn't seen anybody on the street in almost ten blocks but she felt eyes on them the whole way.

From Park street she noticed a distinct darkening of the skin of the passersby but, otherwise, they were just that– passing along on the billion normal errands city dwellers run. Grandmothers and cabbies and hookey-playing kids, all of it was pretty normal until they crossed Birchbriar.

After that it was like the people all got swallowed up into the shadows that seemed strangely more abundant here.

Sure, there was still the occasional passer but now he was almost always male, almost always young and almost always peering out at the world from behind eyes borrowed from the angel of death. Seeing those ancient gazes in faces that young was like something out of a horror show.

Layla liked it about half as much as she liked walking into a bar full of drunk Ivans.

And then there were the streets themselves.

As they passed between them, the car bumping every few feet as it failed to miss a pothole, Layla felt she was seeing the place again for the first time.

It was just barely a city anymore, really. The assembly lines had shut down, the mills closed and their workers displaced or replaced by cheaper foreign labor, the same old story.

Gray Harbor was only a place by default these days, kept so by virtue of its remaining skyscraping bones. The lights were still on in a few places, of course. Cities take decades to die, even small ones like Gray Harbor.

9/11 didn't come close to killing New York. Katrina didn't rub out New Orleans. The riots barely scratched L.A.'s surface.

What ailed Gray Harbor was probably a more fatal condition than any of those in the long run, but not so dramatic. Sure, it was hemorrhaging people and commerce in a steady inexorable flow but the exodus was slow and devoid of fanfare.

The main bus station- Old Central not New Grande- was the disembarkation point of choice for anybody wanting to take a Gray Harbor holiday. There were still people like that, strangely enough, though not nearly as many as those making their exits.

The city still had a semblance of its old nightlife, enough to attract the budget conscious or, more often, those who just wanted someplace to disappear.

There was life in the Downs still and in the C Section, especially on the weekends and Welfare Check Night. There was still motion in the Heights; rich people, like cockroaches, were even harder to kill than cities.

And, of course, there was still money to be made if you were smart enough and had the balls to see something through.

The area around the Towers was like those pictures you saw on the news about life in Belfast or those human warrens in Brazil.

Jumper was always talking about them, how no white people could last in there over night and how the cops left the whole place to the gangs.

The Section might not have been an occupied bit of somebody else's country but, damn it, it sure felt that way.

The fact that Max seemed to agree didn't do much for her nerves. He stopped looking at her and talking altogether the second they passed Birchbriar, transforming instead into a weird combination of guard dog and radar dish. It was like he'd checked his humanity at the border.

She got it. Just a looking out the window there was no way you couldn't.

The neighborhood, if you could call it that, was all the carcasses of old row houses, five to a block with most of their walls in common and made of that old sort of brick that looked like it had spent too much time in somebody's furnace.

These were hollow places now, empty of life or hope but filled with that bottomless chill that the few meager boards nailed across the windows and doors couldn't hope to conceal.

Death trap. Rat trap. Roach trap. Whatever. The place was a people trap and she felt naked and exposed and very much like bolting before he'd got both feet out of the car.

The towers themselves rose up a few blocks ahead, the bastard cross between an alien fortress you'd see in one of those 1950's horror flicks and Pelican fucking Bay.

You couldn't see the windows grills or the grafitti tags from this far off, just the dark shapes and tattoo colors and the seagulls circling the top like vultures. But you damned sure felt the weight of their shadow.

"You want to get moving," he said, half distracted,

like he was sizing up the shadows in the vacant upper windows and the hollows of the nearest doorways and was already forgetting her. "These fools don't play."

She nodded, trying not to look too relieved that he was releasing her.

"You gonna be okay with," she didn't know this guy. She had no idea what he was up to and it stuck in her throat. "With, y'know, whatever?"

"Yeah, yeah," he muttered, even more lost in his scanning and plans than a second previous. Again there was that frost in his eyes, like the icy film on a window over a winter lake. "I'm cool."

She found herself wanting him to say something Clint Eastwood-y like "Take a lot more than them Dogs got to scare me" or "Anybody starts static out here, they gonna get the storm" or something cheesy and brave like that.

But Max wasn't that kind of idiot. It was clear, from the hard, almost hatchet carved quality his face had taken on, that he knew better than she how tough guys ended up in places like this.

"Well," she said, reaching for the key. "Okay then."

He rapped his knuckles twice on the roof of her car (his way of saying good-bye?) and then moved slowly but directly off toward the Towers.

"While it can be described as a collection of bands, the ties that bind a tribe are more complicated. Tribal leadership is personal, not governmental, with "chief's" functioning as people of high influence. Pulling tribe members together for group action is a function of charisma and the manipulation of consensus. The tribe is tied together by structures known as lineages, clan, moieties, and/or phratries. The local groups that compose a traditional tribal society are communal and strongly social, with members linked by kinship."– **FROM INTRO TO SOCIOLOGY 101:, MIDWEST UNIVERSITY PRESS, 1992**

TRACK 7: GANGSTA NATION

The Dogs ran a tight ship. Eleven blocks out from the towers the normal neighborhood traffic disappeared.

The only cars visible were either rusted-out junkers slouching like crumbling statues against the sidewalks or the occasional spotless, perfect SUV, in obligatory blue.

It looked like an abandoned neighborhood with its block after block of boarded windows and doors but that was just camouflage for the cops and the 'heads. Yeah it was dead quiet and nothing moved on the street beyond the odd bit of paper dancing on an anemic breeze but that didn't mean there weren't eyes in there. Every sixth window or door had eyes behind it and Max knew for sure that those eyes were tracking him. They probably didn't know what to make of him (which was keeping him alive) but they were definitely watching.

They had to be wondering just who the hell he thought he was. He wasn't flying a flag, blue or otherwise, and he wasn't strapped that they could see. His time in the desert might have given him the stalking stride of a cop in their eyes but cops didn't have the balls to come into the Section unless they were ten deep and braced in riot gear.

No matter what the mayor told the press, everybody knew who owned the Section. This was Blue Dog country and the Towers were the capitol.

If you knew what to look for you could see that this

was the center of the Section and it was divided into two rings.

The outer ring, what he'd just crossed, was meant to look empty so the uninvited could be tracked.

The second ring was more lively; the sentries were visible there. A few thuggy looking kids lounged on a front stoop, giving him the hard eye as he passed but obviously just as confused by him as their invisible brothers.

They were only there to greet the town cars and beamers that rolled in from Hightown for their daily hit of whatever was on special and he clearly wasn't buying or driving. By the time their brains had worked out they might want to stop him for a quick chat about his intentions, Max had passed them by as well.

If there was one thing he'd learned in the desert it was how to short-circuit a soldier's brain.

He knew getting to the towers was the easy part. Getting through them to the top was something else. Folks called them towers but what they really were was three slabs of layered concrete and glass linked together by a maze of fire escapes and bridges. They'd been built in the 50's as part of some help-the-poor kick one of the mayors was on.

Max couldn't remember the history. He knew they used to call the Towers the *Andrew Johnson Housing Development.* He knew they'd been clean once and the elevators all worked and the lights didn't flicker (those that stayed lit at all) and that they'd sold whole the idea as a way to get people who needed shelter off the streets so they could be "productive," whatever the hell that meant.

What it turned out to be was a cheap and easy way

of getting most of the local blacks confined to a manageable area that the cops could keep their thumbs on without much trouble. It worked for about a decade or so and then the bottom fell out.

The first ever Devil's Night, what the papers called a riot over King's assassination, had shown the cops the truth of that old adage; whoever can destroy something is the one who really owns it.

By the time that first night was done the Towers had their name and one of them was belching black smoke up into the Harbor's overcast sky.

Even before the Dogs came, there was no safety to be found there for anyone after that night. But cops learned pretty quick that entering those buildings was likely the last thing they'd do on this Earth and so they just stopped doing it.

As a kid Max's folks had told him, on pain of ass whipping, to keep himself well clear of the Towers. As a teenager, after a nearly fatal attempt to hook up with Chantrelle Webster who lived on the tenth floor of tower two and whose brothers took a dim view of boys trying to get in her pants, Max had learned his folks were probably right about that after all. Running from those two maniacs down eleven flights of stairs and kicking the door of its hinges at the bottom to get out taught him everything he needed to know about the towers: *Stay the Hell Out.*

Things only got worse when the Dogs moved in. Seeing the place as a perfect fortress, complete with all the rooms they wanted for their business operations and their harems, Top Dog himself moved into Tower One and took over the top floor.

The Dogs had tried to recruit Max right about then.

he was nine and some older kid in brand new Chucks, jeans and gortex jacket had offered him a couple of fifties to just run a package around the corner to his man real quick like.

Max didn't bite but Lavall did and started that day on the ground floor of Blue Dog Inc.

He would never be Top Dog. You had to be from Cali to get that nod. But, over the next decade, during which he kept avoiding both the cops and the bullets of rivals, Lavall rose to the rank of Third Dog, adviser to the Top. Lavall was always smart.

Not like Justine or even Max himself but smart in that way an old fat sewer rat is smart enough to avoid traps and gas and poison and eat to his heart's content.

Lavall was up there, on one of the top three floors so that was where Max had to get.

He passed through the narrow front door, an obvious fire hazard that would force a fatal bottle neck if too many tried to get out at one time. The first corridor was dark, as expected and covered with so many tags they had merged into a weird spray-painted tessellation of letters and color that reminded Max of something he'd seen on the wall of the old imperial palace before they'd mortared it to bits. Nobody lived down here so the only doors were for the elevator and the stairwell.

"Yeah," he said to himself as he scanned the ugly dark maw of the lift. "Not that stupid yet, son."

He took the stairs down to the maintenance level.

There had to be a good twenty Dogs on the floors between him and Lavall. More, if you counted the ass kissers and the bed toys.

Each of them would have at least one gun handy, a

Glock or Tech Nine being most likely.

The sentries might have been short circuited by him but the Dogs who actually stayed in the tower had only one job: take out anybody the top dog hadn't told them was invited.

"Take out" for good.

There'd be no short-circuits there, just a tap to the head or the neck or chest and the end of Max forever.

Nope. Not going out quite like that, he thought. *At least, not today.*

If there was ammonia or something like it down on the maintenance level and if the Tower used central air, Max would be seeing Lavall, all right, but nobody but Lavall would see him.

The maintenance level was also the laundry level and the garbage level. You passed through the concrete room with the dilapidated washers and dryers- five of each- through the garbage room that was supposed to be just for paper goods (but was just an underground dump) to the room with the cleaning fluids and extra fuses and the vents in the walls that led up and through the whole tower.

There were Dog tags all over, threatening pain and death for anyone who wasn't one and found themselves on their turf. Max winced looking at the hastily scrawled AKAs– *Boney* and *Twist, Hardboy* and *Mutt, Devil69* and, of course, *TOP.*

The tags were shit, nothing like the ornate and colorful works of the bomb squads of his childhood. They were just chicken-scratched note cards that might as well have said *Killroy was here* for all the value they had. They were as empty as the people who'd made them but would last longer down there in the concrete depths.

Those original "vandals" weren't. Not to Max. To him the original graffiti bombers had been, well, something he still didn't have a name for. Not heroes exactly and certainly not saints.

Watching two of the crews beat each other bloody over the right to bomb the three stories of virgin brick behind *Keelie's Market* had shown they weren't much different than him.

But they were different. Something in those boys had told them the response to a world that kicked at them constantly was not to kick back but to inject some beauty, to *make* something, to *hope.* The real world might well be grey but they weren't going to help darken it.

Max admired those boys and, though he didn't realize it, was shaped by their works as much as the sides of the buildings and trucks they painted. More maybe.

It made him sick to see what was left of their art but there was nothing he could do about it, even if there was time, which there wasn't.

The maintenance room was shut behind a rickety, vented door that seemed to hang on its hinges out of habit more than anything else. Once there had probably been a need for a key to get the thing open but the handle had long since been pounded away. Now there was just a small black hole.

Max reached his fingers inside, feeling the last of the remaining tumblers, greasy and dusty from decades of neglect and abuse. He flexed his index, twisted with his thumb. The door opened with a small, almost grateful, click and he was inside.

The desert had taught him a lot of things, especially about bombs. There were all kinds and not all of them were, in themselves, lethal. Some of them just made a loud distracting noise; some of them just made smoke.

The sand people earned his grudging respect at their ability to make these things out of whatever seemed to be lying around.

More than that, they tweaked his curiosity so that, when they actually managed to take a prisoner and that prisoner was lucid enough to talk he would ask about how it was done. Anything to pass the time, right?

Minutes stretched out like lifetimes between firefights and there were a lot of minutes in the desert.

The Dogs had probably broken in here, found nothing worth taking or using to cook whatever they were selling to the hypes and fiends, and left it all to gather dust. There were cans of ancient paint, thinner to go with them, grease, cleansers and a few other liquids he hadn't expected but which would be helpful nonetheless. There was even a stack of aluminum roller pans, perfect for hat he had in mind. The ventilation fans turned slowly in their tubes, dusty but working. Perfect.

Max smiled. If any of those fools upstairs would have listened up in chem class or even took the time to understand how the top floors could stay cool in the summer and warm in the winter without an expensive AC system, they might have been prepared for the party he was about to give them.

But they didn't and they weren't and there was somebody here he had to talk to.

It took about ten minutes to get the stuff mixed.

When it came down to it, he chose the empty paint cans over the roller pans. He needed a lot of smoke and he needed as much of it to go up, rather than out, as possible.

The cans' shapes would do that. Good.

The stink from his little concoctions told him he'd got the mixture right so all there as left was to set the fires.

Always seems to come down to this, he thought with rue.

He cracked his little silver Zippo, lit up the ancient cardboard paper towel roll he scrounged from the garbage room and lit each of the cans in succession. Holding his jacket over his face, he bolted from the little room and checked his watch.

The smoke wouldn't reach the top floors. Hell, by the time it got halfway up it would be little more than ugly fumes, but that would be enough to get the rank and file panicking and more than enough to get those upstairs curious as to what the hell was going on below.

Lavall was smart so he'd send some of his little doggies out to check if this was some kind of an attack while the rest of the idiots poured down the fires escapes.

With a little luck he'd have the place to himself, mostly, in about ten minutes.

He tipped out to the bottom of the stairwell and listened and, sure enough, there was already some screaming and running around going on up there. Two minutes later you'd have thought they'd let a heard of angry buffalo loose in Tower One. It wasn't true but he could swear he felt the building shake from all that stampeding fear.

Four minutes in, the noise had dipped a bit, meaning most of them were outside now and he just had to wait for the little bloodhounds to make their way down to investigate...

There it was. Two pairs of footfalls clanking softly on the steel steps heading down, not out. Good old Lavall.

It didn't take much to put them down. They were just teenagers, big as they were, and they weren't really looking for a fight down there. Puppies more than actual Dogs. Odds were Lavall had told them to look for a short or a garbage fire or something. One of them was sill in his pajama bottoms. Jesus.

Before they realized they weren't alone Max had smashed the bigger one's face into the cinderblock wall enough times to put him back to sleep. The smaller one managed a yelp of surprised before Max's boot tapped his solar plexus and sat him down.

"Lavall still live here?" said Max, crouching down to hear any reply that might come between the wheezes.

The puppy shook his head weakly but it was stupid. They both knew Max could see he was lying.

"Yeah, he do," he said and placed his palm on the puppy's sternum. "What room?"

Again the puppy tried to front some bullshit response but Max was on the clock.

"Gonna need that door number, kid," he said.

He pressed in on the boy's sternum, further cutting off his ability to take in air. He only had to ask one more time before he got the straight answer.

"Good dog," he said. Then he cracked the kid's

head against the wall and set him, sleeping, beside his brother.

He had another five minutes before the crowds realized the building wasn't burning down and somebody came looking for these two. Just enough to get what he wanted from Lavall.

It didn't surprise Max that the elevators still worked. The doors might look like broke down tagged up sheets of rusty steel but that was for show. Top Dog didn't walk no thirty-eight flights to get to his crib, baby. And everybody who lived in the Tower knew better than to risk using his personal conveyance. But that was under normal conditions.

Nobody was dumb enough to use them to get out during what as supposed to be a fire but that didn't mean he couldn't use them to go up.

As he rose past each floor he could see a little of the hallways that lay on the other side of the small circle of glass that served as the elevator's window.

The first twenty were pretty identical, just ugly, barely livable apartment floors. There had been carpets once, maybe, but they'd long since been stripped or worn away. The doors were likewise just remnants of their original status– no longer colored or numbered but, he was sure, easy to find for whoever still lived there.

It wasn't much different than he remembered from the one time he'd been there all those years ago but, of course, the lower floors were just for the pack.

From twenty-one up things improved visibly from floor to floor. The low twenties, what he could see through the little window, were set aside for the soldiers, Little Dogs mostly, what the news people called gang bangers.

The upper twenties were for merchandising and cooking. Lots of the walls had been knocked out, destroying even the idea of apartment life implied by the front facade.

What was left was an open area, like a sweatshop he guessed, with long tables and stoves and scales. The factory floors.

The dogs did good business in everything that was smokable or shootable or even, in Lavall's case, fuckable.

Doubtful the corner strollers were kept here. Too much potential for drama.

The low thirties were apartments again, this time looking, if not quite new, then certainly more like places human beings might want to stay. The doors had paint and little silver numbers. The walls were dingy but intact.

Thirty-five even had a rug.

Those floors were for the Big Dogs- the crew leaders and Top's muscle. He couldn't see them but he knew there were all kinds of weapons stockpiled behind each of those doors, all clean and loaded and ready to do business if Top told the owner somebody needed to go.

No fun coming back through a full house if he couldn't get done with Lavall fast enough. He'd be walking down then, definitely meeting up with some folks on their way back after the false alarm. He had to be on the ground before they got back to their guns. And that presumed that each one hadn't scooped up his favorite before heading out, *just in case.*

The bell still worked too. And the little lights

behind the numbers. Thirty-seven was the stop. The doors slid apart and he stepped out.

This floor looked as if it had just been painted, just had the new carpets laid. There were only two doors, one on either side of the hall, one for each of the Under Dogs, Two and Three. Technically you could say they were both number Two but their jobs made the distinction for them.

Lavall was Three because he looked after the cash flow. Whoever held the Two spot was in charge of hurting anybody Top wanted hurt, whoever, however, wherever.

Funny thing though: Number Two was not home. His door was open. His over-cranked sound system was still pumping out something low and slow but he was O-U-T.

If he was lucky, if he was smart, he was out with the Top, watching that back. If not, if he'd bolted with the rest at the smell of smoke, well, that would probably mean Lavall was in for a promotion.

Laval's door, the one with the number the puppy had given him, was still closed.

Max knocked and waited.

"Who that?" came the familiar voice from inside. Years hadn't changed it at all.

"Fire department," said Max.

The door opened and a wiry man in a wifebeater and long khaki shorts appeared. His hair was in the same perfectly even rows Max remembered but they were long now, eight years longer, and trailing down his back.

He had a goatee now and a lot more muscle on him than Max expected (never smart to get soft in this

106

business and Lavall was always smart). His skin was the same polished cedar color Max remembered too only now there was the face of a pitbull burned into one shoulder with three vertical lines under the collar– Third Dog status.

"You got bigger," he said after he'd looked Max over.

"You too," said Max.

They stood there looking at each other, weighing the years they'd spent together and apart, deciding what they should do about all that, if anything.

Max could still smell the faint wisps of his smoke explosion hanging in the air and, over Lavall's shoulder, he could see the blood-colored walls and dark mahogany furniture of Third Dog's front room.

There was definitely a gun behind the door somewhere, maybe even in the hand Max couldn't see. If Lavall wanted, he could lay Max out here and, by dark, there wouldn't even be a stain on the floor. If he'd come looking for trouble Lavall would have smelled it and that's how it would have been.

But Max wasn't looking for trouble. Not directly.

"It's Reggie, ain't it?" he said after a time. Max nodded. Of course it was. "Well, get in here, nigga. You got about five minutes for me to decide if I'm walking you out of this piece or you trying to make it on your lone."

"Lone is fine," said Max, not giving up anything.

Lavall smiled, even chuckled a little. "Same old Max," he said.

Then he shut the door.

There was almost nothing to their conversation, just

the kind of small talk that might pass between people who had worked at a fast food place for a decade together but never said more than two words in all that time.

"You look good, yo."

"What can I say?"

Eight years later and there just wasn't much. They both knew

Max was lucky to still be breathing and they both knew Lavall could have put the heat on him any time he wanted during that long vacation. Max didn't know why Lavall never gave him up. It wasn't for old times sake, that was for sure. Lavall was about as sentimental as the GPS in his old Bradley. Yeah, they had been friends, come up together like people say, but that was the past. In the Here and Now Lavall was all business. There was only one reason he would have kept Max's survival a secret: there was something in it for him, an angle.

"So, Reggie, huh," said Lavall. Max kept still and hung as close to the exit as was possible without coming off rude. "Okay. I figured that would be the thing to pull your ass back here one day or another."

"So?" said Max after a time.

"Yeah," said Lavall. "Maybe I'll hook you up. Might could get a show out of that. These little dogs could use a wake up too. Some of 'em is getting soft."

"Got two napping in the basement right now," said Max.

Chuckling, Lavall drifted off, moving past the leather upholstered couches and the 40s retro-style floor lamps into the kitchen area.

It was all white tile and sparkly clean appliances.

BETTER ANGELS

Like the rest of the place, you could eat off of any surface. Lavall was always clean like that.

Everything, from the wall-sized plasma screen to the polished mahogany bookshelves and coffee tables to the thousand thread count curtains, looked like it had just come out of the box.

Max doubted Lavall touched any of it for one second longer than he absolutely had to. The place was like somebody's cartoon notion of the home of a successful player from the square world.

Lavall's idea of success was a life-sized dollhouse and him as Ken and Barbie. Or, maybe, there was something more. Maybe this was all for show and Lavall had his mind on something completely else.

The water came on and Max heard him washing his hands. "So that smoke was all you, right? This place ain't fixing to burn down?"

Of course not. But Lavall obviously thought it was funny that Max had been playing with fire again. He finished up in the sink and returned with a couple of sodas in bottles.

Max declined. He was ticking off the minutes in head. The other Dogs were likely already sniffing around downstairs. If somebody decided to go down instead of up...

Lavall shrugged, clicked the bottles together in one hand and spread himself out on the sofa. His trainers looked like they'd just been stitched together and handed off to him in the last ten minutes. Clean.

The coffee table he set them on had to come out of one of them upscale catalogues. Nobody in the Section sold that type of shit. All of Lavall's furniture was like that: dark simulations of old wood and older designs-

109

the kind of thing one of them swells from the heights might fill up their cribs with. Yeah, Lavall had aspirations.

"Oh, yes," he said, catching Max's appraising glance around the room. "Your boy done come up in the world, huh?"

"Bet you feel like you could go higher," said Max, blandly. Lavall knocked back the first soda, belched and said, "Maybe. Maybe not."

"Same old Lavall," said Max.

"Nah, nigga," said the other, fumbling around for the system remote. "Older and wiser. New and improved."

He found it and clicked on the massive television, riffling through channels until he found a cartoon he liked: Hawk vs Weasel or something. He settled back into the accommodating leather and sipped at the second bottle.

Max waited, showing nothing but still tick-tick-ticking away in his head.

"Reggie, huh?" said Lavall after the third vignette of the hawk getting his beak blown off by some high tech weasel gadget.

"Yeah."

"Okay, then," said Lavall. "Listen."

He told Max what he needed to know then Third Dog put his arm around him, walked him to the elevator, rode down with him and walked him out, all under the confused and interested glares of the many Dogs, Puppies and Bitches that made the tower home.

"You owe me for this," he said into Max's ear before backing away. "You know that, right?"

Max knew. As long as he saw Reggie in the next

twenty-four hours, owing Lavall a favor was a tiny price. Anything was.

"All right then, nigga," said Lavall, loud enough for the pack to hear. "Get on like you been shit on. And don't come 'round here no more, 'less you want to get rolled up."

Max started walking.

"I must eat my dinner. This island's mine, by Sycorax my mother, Which thou takest from me. When thou camest first, Thou strokedst me and madest much of me, wouldst give me Water with berries in't, and teach me how To name the bigger light, and how the less, That burn by day and night: and then I loved thee And show'd thee all the qualities o' the isle, The fresh springs, brine-pits, barren place and fertile: Cursed be I that did so! All the charms Of Sycorax, toads, beetles, bats, light on you! For I am all the subjects that you have, Which first was mine own king: and here you sty me In this hard rock, whiles you do keep from me The rest o' the island." – **CALIBAN, from THE TEMPEST by William Shakespeare**

TRACK 8: ANGRY JOHNNY

The walls were white and not that perfect pristine white that made you think of chalk or peppermint gum or the teeth in a beautiful smile.

No, these walls were dingy white, once-white, the white of a butcher's smock, all pocked and mottled by time and the spill from his duties.

Bruno hated butchers. His old poppa was a butcher and a beater and shit-kicking sonofabitch but mostly a he was butcher. He slaughtered cows and pigs, cut them up into bits and sold them to grandmas and aunties under cute little names like *prime* or *top* or *shank*.

He stank of old blood and lies and, when he got enough hooch in him he stank of Bruno, of his fear inspired piss and the spray of blood that erupted when Ol' Poppa's fists connected.

Ol' Poppa called it *tenderizing,* what he did to him on those ugly nights, called it *getting him set for the Harbor.*

"Y'ain't got the brains God gave a bucket of silt," he would say on those evenings when there was only beer in the house and not enough to do more than buzz him. "So, you better get tough boy and that right quick."

Bruno was a slow study but he did get it eventually. He got bigger than anybody expected, faster than anybody predicted and, when his Ol' Poppa pushed past what 15 year old Bruno realized was the limit, well, that was the end of Ol' Poppa.

The cops called it self-defense. Everybody on Gabon St. knew for years what that father had done to that son. They all whispered and pointed and shook their heads but they never once lifted a finger until Bruno used all ten of his to put Ol' Poppa down. By then it was too late for both of them.

They probably felt a little bit guilty watching the cops load him up so, even though this time there hadn't been any screaming or begging from son to father to just please stop, they all swore up and down that the old man had just gone berserk.

What was the boy to do?

Never mind that the boy was already pushing six feet and could carry twice his own weight for ten blocks without breaking a sweat or losing wind.

Never mind, when the cops got the wrong impression of the incident and came at him with their nightsticks that the typhoon of blows seemed to pass over him wholly unnoticed.

Never mind all of that. Ol' Poppa had finally got his and the folks on Galen St. just couldn't let him go down for the giving.

It was like all those times they listened or watched got stored up like a stack of get-out-of-jail-free cards, just for that inevitable day when he paid Ol' Poppa back.

He spent all of twelve hours in stir before the badges came to let him go. He sat in the corner of the big steel cage, left totally alone by the hard and intoxicated men who shared the space.

Halfway through the night of them scrapping and wining and pissing themselves, one of the overnighters noticed his hands were still covered in Ol' Poppa's blood.

"Hey, man," he said. "You wanna clean them guns off before they process you. Get blood on their little print book and that's your ass."

That was Nicky. The guy Bruno ended up thrashing almost to death never gave his name but he did make the mistake of calling him shit-for-brains. That was nothing anyone was ever calling Bruno again. Not stupid, not fuckhead, not dimwit not nothing on that list or there would be hell to pay.

The pounding was over so fast the guards barely noticed a "fight" had happened. Of course nobody in the cell saw how it went.

Then the cops came down, said he was free to go and that was pretty much the end of it. There was a- what did they call it– a hearing about how he'd done in Ol' Poppa but it was over quick what with all those witnesses stepping up on his side.

Ol' Poppa was a true monster and poor Bruno had not caught him unawares in the kitchen, sleeping off a case of beer. He hadn't smacked him in the back of the head with that big iron skillet that Ol' Poppa called *Pancake Joe.*

He hadn't carried his dazed father into the front room of their little old house and pounded his face, over and over and over and over and over and over, into the sturdy oak front door jam until he heard his neck crack. Bruno was good boy who only defended himself against that evil sadistic monster. Poor kid.

Mr. Lenderhoff helped him get a job working security at Marston's Discount. Mrs. Heller made sure he got his groceries in those first few weeks. With Ol'

Poppa out of the picture and him turning eighteen the week after there was no more need even to pretend about school. Bruno was free and life, if wasn't good exactly, well it wasn't hell either.

A couple years after that Nicky showed up again, dripping with cash and offered him a better job. He was one of those guys that was hooked up with the Ivans and he was always flush.

"You come work for me and you can quit with the rent-a-cop shit," he said. "Shit, the real cops won't fuck with you either."

Bruno told him the real cops always treated him pretty square, calling him Big Man and telling him he out to think about joining the force. He did look into it but the written test was too hard. His head started hurting on the second page so he just walked out.

The first gig was collections. People owed and people needed to be reminded about keeping their promises. Niki would talk and Bruno would stand there and they mostly coughed up something. Usually it was money. When they couldn't then, after Bruno took a turn, it was blood and then money.

Bruno had a hard time with it at first. He might look like that big monster from the movies without the green skin and the soldiers chasing him everywhere but he wasn't really into hurting people who didn't do wrong by him personally.

Nicky caught the problem and told him just put Ol' Poppa's face on anybody he had to hit and he did and then it was okay.

And that's how it went for a couple years, with Nicky turning out to be right about both the money and the cops. Bruno had fat pockets, a good friend and nobody ever, ever called him stupid, anymore. Everything was Jake as Jake could be until Layla showed up.

From he first time he saw her, dancing drunk on Nicky's table, swinging her ass and her hair back and forth like a whipsaw, just barely half in the jeans and Black Flag tee shirt she always wore back then, Bruno had it out for her.

He was always hot when she was around, his clothes always feeling too tight. He couldn't put two words together in front of her even though she would always talk to him so sweet.

Nicky always had a string of girls on him, *bed heaters* he called them. They would stick for a few days, a few nights really, and then hit the bricks, disappearing like the empty boxes of Chinese or pizza that Nicky shared with them.

Sometimes he'd make one of them sex Bruno up because, according to Nicky, that's how you treat your boys: share the wealth. Bruno liked sex but he didn't always like it when they would put on those fake smiles or, worse, cry when Nicky sent them his way.

He hated those smiles more than the tears. God damn, how he hated those fake smiles. Those smiles always meant they thought he was just some big dumb animal, something they had to get through just to please Nicky.

It was a struggle sometimes for him not to end some of those girls and put them where they put the people who really couldn't pay. That was all over when Layla showed up.

Nicky stopped answering his phone, stopped coming around except when he had a job, stopped bringing in random heaters for his bed. Bruno missed him and his jokes, hated how quiet his life got when Nicky wasn't in it. But, Layla made it okay.

One night, about two am, Bruno got tired of bouncing off Nicky's voicemail, he just walked over to *The Waterfront* and peeked in though the break in the curtains there.

They were *doing it* in there, he knew it. They always were. All Nicky wanted to do anymore was Layla and, watching her ride him, all sweaty and serious in the half dark, like it was the only thing in the world she wanted and the only place in the word worth being, Bruno understood why. He wished he was Nicky. The way she was, everybody wished that.

He watched them, her, for an hour while she did everything to his friend. One time he swore she saw him too. She looked up, just for no reason and, to Bruno anyway, it seemed she looked right into him, freezing him on the spot.

He went away then, back to being twelve and waiting for Ol Poppa to fall asleep so he could have some safety and peace. The moment passed and she was all about tasting as much of Nicky as she could fit.

He went home then, quiet and happy and not worried anymore about Nicky disappearing. He understood. Layla was the place to be, if she would let you in. Layla was heaven and Disneyland and Nicky was lucky to get in and ride.

And she was so sweet. She always talked to him and not because Nicky told her. Her smile went to the bone. She called him Bruno the Bear and he liked it. She called him "honey" and it was like he was bathing in it when she did.

When the Ivans moved Nicky up in the crew and he started making plans for the big grab, he would disappear for weeks. During those times Layla would come over or can cook for him or watch cable or play SNIPER FORCE.

She would pass on the stuff Nicky wanted him to do when Nicky couldn't get clear to do it. Best of all, sometimes, just sometimes, she would touch him. Nothing like the way she did Nicky, of course, never anything like that. It would just be her moving past him to the kitchen and her bare shoulder would press into his chest or, while they were watching a scary movie, she'd grab his hand, just for a second and set him on fire.

One time she kissed him good-bye on his cheek and he couldn't get to the bathroom fast enough.

Layla and Nicky were the family he prayed for when Ol' Poppa was on him, people who loved him and treated him right and, if he couldn't be what Nicky was to her, he was happy to just be around her just to bask in her silvery glow.

But the walls, the once-white, the still pocked, the ugly, were making him nervous. He was sure she said he shouldn't go to the *Number One Motel* but to hole up at *Johnston's Residential.* Or was it Nicky who had said that? Or did he just mix it all up himself? No one had called him to say what was up and it was way past the time when they should.

He couldn't call them. Both Layla and Nicky had made that clear. Once the plan got going, he had to stay under until one of them came to get him. He had to sit on the money and the H and not let ANYBODY

GEOFFREY THORNE

touch it or even know about it.

But it was hours since he'd seen or heard from them. It was last night, wasn't it? So a whole day almost since--

And the walls made him think of Ol' Poppa which made him want to hit something which he couldn't do so he did the one thing he'd found that could calm him down when he got this way.

He pulled the black marker out of his bag and popped open the cap. He would wait. Yeah. Of course. Nicky was cool and smart and Layla was sweet and one of them would come for him and then they could take the loot and go somewhere hot and sunny.

He just needed to keep his mind cool until then and he knew how.

He walked over to the nearest wall and started writing on it with the marker, her name, her name, over and over and over.

"East coast cities aren't designed like the rest of the country. Most of them are from before there even was a USA. So, when you see New York city, what you don't see is that it's really fifteen New York city's, each one built on top of the last. And all the people? They're on top of each other too. Yeah, they have neighborhoods, boroughs, whatever they call it, but they're also all over each other. Living together. Living with each other. And you feel it. It's vibrant. Alive. But you go west and things get different. Our cities are designed, mostly so cars can get around in them. They intend to keep people away from each other. New York, DC, Philly, those are horse-and-carriage cities. Los Angeles, San Diego, they're car cities. People live in bubbles, move around in little bubbles. They never have to get along for more than five minutes at a time. It's no shock these people rioted last month. The real surprise is that they don't riot every month." – **FATHER EDUARDO AGUILERA – on LOCAL LATINS, A TV MAGAZINE in 1992**

TRACK 9: OTHERSIDE

She saw him before he saw her, coming back across Harcourt Street with that same look of granite in his eyes.

He'd been gone just long enough that she had begun to wonder maybe if he really didn't have the juice she'd first thought which made her wonder about her prospects for the rest of the day and with Nicky which made her think, *Fuck it. I can stick around a while longer.*

She was always waiting lately, for a slap or a fuck or just some God damned info and she fucking hated it but there wasn't anything else to do.

No way in hell was she going in there after him. No way she'd make it far if she tried.

The Dogs always played with their food before eating and she had no interest in becoming a snack. Bigger and tougher than Max had been chewed up and spit out by the Towers.

Even the Ivans didn't poke their noses in. But here he was, dead-eyed, hard-faced and walking, marching almost, like the last survivor of the worst world war who was still on the lookout for one more good scrap.

Perfect, she thought, catching him catching sight of her. *Fucking perfect.*

He came up next to her, sitting on the SUCK IT, HATERS tag and asked what the hell she was still doing here.

This was exactly the kind of reckless, stupid shit

that could get somebody rolled up or worse. Even a chick.

"No shit, Dr. Watson," she said, sliding down and running one set of fingers under the lip of the hood. "But my engine's being a little bitch so what was I supposed to–?"

There was the sound of that anemic little click- the latch coming free- and then the hood was up an she was bent over it, making a show of both her ass in those jeans and rummaging around in the car's guts.

After ten seconds of watching one or the other he leaned in beside her and said, "Move."

"Hey, thanks, man," she said and meant to go on except that he picked that second to shoot her that same icy look of his, the one that said he wasn't close to trusting a single word she popped out, and she shut it. Spreading out a bit across the exposed engine, he used his hip to get between her and the car.

It wasn't quite a shove but it wasn't particularly gentle either. *Just get out of the way, lady.* His body seemed to say. *Because I'm just about done with all your shit.*

She backed off, smiling quietly.

That scowly expression of his had shown enough for her to find it familiar.

As unpleasant as it was to see, she was happy to have it. It was good to know that this guy was more than the deep sucking well he put on.

It gave her something on which to hang her appraisal, meaning she was that much closer to getting a handle on him. Once she had the handle, the rest was cake.

Watching him rummage around the car's guts her

mind scampered back to the times she'd first sussed what made each of her horses tick. Jumper had been easy.

He wanted things simple and light and fun so all she had to do was keep anything complex or sticky from touching him. It helped that he wasn't the brightest bulb in the lamp and he did make up for his shortcomings.

God, how he made up for them.

Carlos was trickier. He had that macho Cubano thing going, pure Little Havana; sort of like Nicky but with an odd catechism of deeply wounded pride that had to have been read off the back of his father's hand.

He ran icy when he was cold and like lava when he was hot but, if you knew how to massage the ego, to tell him how stellar he was at exactly the perfect second, in just the honeyest tone, well, every guy was as putty as any other.

Carlos smelled like cocoa butter.

Mario didn't and he wasn't nearly as much of a maze but he wasn't as interesting either. He definitely had none of Jumper's flavor. Looking back she wasn't exactly sure why he'd got the nod.

Johnny Boy was little more than a puppy– happy, open as a new toy box, close to rich and pleasantly energetic– a great forgettable ride that was the perfect set-up for Nicky.

Rollercoaster, rape- murder Nicky.

She knew, the very first time seeing him across dance floor of that dive-y Ivan club Francie had dragged her to, that he was a cab to the morgue waiting for a fare.

What the hell was it about the dead boys that drew her so?

Whatever it was, Nicky was made of it; wicked hot, in that strung-out dockworker way, he was connected and he had other vaguely Jumper-ish qualities that made surfing the ebb and flow of his moods worth it.

Even without all that there was the big Plan and the Escape.

Anything, anyone that could take Layla out of this grinding ugly life could make a syphilitic monkey into the sexy hot ticket.

Nicky had a hair trigger, yeah, but if you massaged it just right...

And, now, big Max. Dangerous, bottomless, brick-thick Max. Tasty.

Funny how she was already folding him into her mental harem. He wasn't quite converted yet, no, but she could see him there, easy.

She had a lot more chipping to do to unlock whatever was under the asphalt façade but there was promise showing through the little cracks she'd made.

A little longer, she was sure, and she'd have him knocked. He might be a big stone mountain but she was a girl who could climb if she had to and, just now, she really did.

"Looks fine to me," he said, snapping her back to the moment.

The way he was draped over the engine it looked like he was going to climb inside. Thorough.

She liked that. He was like a dog with a leftover shank once he got going, no matter how small the bone might be. It was another tell and she thought it was Good. Not quite the handle but almost.

"I don't know what's wrong with her," she said, wistfully. "She just gets pissy like this sometimes. I think-"

Max held up a hand for quiet.

"Get in," he said without looking up. "Start it."

"What? Already? No way."

"Get in and start it," he said.

She gave him a quizzical little look and sauntered around to the driver's side where she fought with the door a bit before sliding in.

She reminded herself to replace the beads in the seat cover when she got a chance; the current batch didn't do much to give her the advertised *soft massage* but did a job of scratching into her back right through the fabric of her tee shirt.

"Ready?" he might have said something but the city noise and the vehicle's metal bulk ate it. She heard him rap three times on the side of the car, hard, and took it as a signal to try the engine.

It grumbled a bit, prickly about being forced back to work after such a nice rest, but it quickly turned over and settled into the familiar mechanical growl she'd come to know.

"Omigod!" she yelled over the growl. "You did it. I can't believe you fucking-"

She actually had a good two minutes more of telling him how awesome he was but she was cut short by the sight of his dark shadow passing her window, walking the other way.

She called out to him, twice, before it penetrated that he was leaving her behind. She was out of the car in a tick, trotting after him. That stride of his was like something out of a war movie and she hated him a little for making her chase.

"Hey!" she said, wheezing from the sprint. "What the hell?" He kept moving. "Dude! Hey! MAX!"

It was no use. He kept walking and she kept trotting to keep up. It wouldn't have been so bad, maybe, if she hadn't been smoking for ten years and if she hadn't only just given it up.

Her lungs were on fire after fifty steps but she couldn't let him go. She kept talking, questioning, joking, almost begging, anything to get him to stop and pay attention. Finally she simply collapsed to her hands and knees on the pavement.

"Max," she said between hacks and wheezes. "Max, please."

She watched him continue down the block, unable to rise from the embarrassing position and unable to stop the damned coughing.

"Those things'll kill you," she remembered Jumper telling her over and over. Then she would light up, open her shirt and let her blue star shut down the conversation.

She wondered if he'd be happy to see how close to right he'd actually been. *Poor Jumper. Poor Layla.*

The coughing stopped at just about the time the big black boots appeared on the sidewalk in front of her.

"You okay?" he said, somewhere above. Then there was a hand on her shoulder and another on her arm and she was rising, mostly without effort.

"Yeah," she said, shrugging his big stony fingers away. "Yeah, I'm good."

He gave her a quick scan, the same hard cold stare he'd put on Nicky back at the *Mercy,* and then he turned to go.

No! Her hand shot out and took hold of his arm before she could stop it. It was a mistake, a stupid intrusion into his personal space, but it was too late. Idiot! He stopped and turned slowly back towards her.

"What," he said.

The hand retreated and Layla stifled the shudder that wanted to run through her. He was still wild after all and, big as he was, riding this bronco could get a girl banged up good.

"Look," she dragged a stray bang across her face, letting the edges linger on her upper lip as they passed. "What's up? I thought we were cool."

He went on saying nothing, just looking at her face as if it was a TV screen and the show was something called *Layla's Every Little Thought.*

"Is it because I didn't ghost out of here like you told me?" she said, going in instead of giving in to the urge to just chuck it and go. "Because I told you my car's a little bitch. You should have seen the shot she put me through this morning. Took me almost an hour to get out of the freaking parking lot."

"I look like a mark to you?" said Max, cutting her off.

"What?" she said, just so horribly aghast at the suggestion. "No! Why would you even–?"

"You been working me since the *Mercy,"* he said. "Trying to."

"'Work' you," she said. "Work what? Work how? I was just trying to-"

He was close to her then, suddenly and not in a good way, not in a way that promised hot sheets or a gentle hand.

It was the tiniest sliver of the show he'd given

Nicky last night and Layla was grateful it was only that. It was chilly in Max's shadow and she wasn't dressed for the weather.

"You think this is Fuck With Max Day?" he said in a low, menacing whisper. "I ain't no fucking mark."

"No," she said, fixing her eyes on his, willing him to see the truth. "'course not. No way."

"Not for you, not for nobody," he said. "You get that, smart girl?"

She sputtered something, trying to get a rhythm going, trying to find another way in and failing again.

This guy was becoming more than Everest. He was morphing into fucking Olympus Mons and she wasn't sure she was up to the climb after all. It didn't matter anyway. He never let her settle in.

"What's wrong with the car?" he said.

"What? Shit, I don't know."

"What's wrong with the car?" he said.

"Well, fuck," she said, looking for a smile, still spinning for him. "Nothing now, right? You fixed it."

When he turned abruptly and started off again it was as if someone had turned the sun back on. Her face got warm, hot even and she felt a weird tingle in her fingertips.

"Okay," she called after him. "Okay. You're right. Just stop, okay. You're right."

One time with Nicky, early on, before she'd got all his twists and turns mapped out in her head, he'd sent her to the moon.

It wasn't the first blast off ever but it was by far the best. He flexed something, bent her leg just so, gripped her nape in just the perfect way and, just for a second, every ugly thing in her life had vanished in a flash of shuddering white.

After, after he'd gone and she'd had time to process, she'd realized that the glorious moment had less to do with Nicky's talents and more to do with her dropping her guard just long enough for him to ring the bell.

It was a lesson and she learned it.

Never again.

So Layla was as shocked as anybody when the truth just spilled out of her, for him, in that same satisfying, skin-tightening climax.

Of *course* there was nothing really wrong with the car. She'd pulled the fuel line. Not all the way, no, just enough to keep the engine from firing up. She wanted Max to feel she needed him, his help, his protection and, since he was on his own business, she needed to put a fine point on it or risk letting him go.

Nicky was shit-crazy, too quick with his fists on the best day, certainly still wicked pissed off from his late night humiliation at Max's hands.

Until she figured out her next move she was safer under the granite wing of old stone face than anywhere else she could think of.

"Yeah," he said. Layla thought she saw another crack in the armor there. "Yeah, okay. But, shit. Why not just ask me?"

"Do you know me?" she said. "Do you trust me? I'm fucking desperate here, Max. Jesus. I hadda do something."

She watched him think to over. Was she lying? Was she greasing him for something? Was any of her pleading actually true? He was a cagey sonofabitch, no doubt.

Then she saw his scanning eyes fall on the shiner Nicky had given her, the one even an extra layer of foundation couldn't quite hide and she knew she had him.

"Yeah," he said, softly, almost human again. "Yeah, I guess I can see that."

She launched herself at him then, hanging on his neck like it was the edge of a cliff.

She thanked him, crying *I'm sorry's* into his chest until he finally had to nudge her away. The gentleness of his push told her the tears had been a good touch. She wiped them off with the heel of her hand.

"So, y'know," she said, not yet quite able to look at him square. "I can still drive you around while you do your business. No charge."

"'No charge,' huh?" he said with an odd rumble under the words.

Was that a chuckle? No fucking way.

"Shit," she said, looking up and seeing it. "Is that a smile? Careful. You might crack your face."

"Just get in the damned car, smart girl," he said, already moving back toward it. "I ain't got all day for this."

•••

Leaving the Section behind was like being kicked out of the free clinic after being told the sores on your gums were just the result of too much lemonade.

Layla rolled down her window and had to fight the urge to hang her head out in the breeze like that dog in the hotel commercial.

You smell that, boy? That's a Heartshore Vacation.

But she didn't. Max might be sleeping in her back yard now but he wasn't eating from her hand. Not yet.

She shot a quick eye his way to take the temperature of his mood. He was folded back into himself, shock, watching the buildings and people blur past outside the way those Tarot card scammers scrutinized the deck.

The difference was she could tell he was actually looking for something in the blur of faces and facades while the scammers were just looking for a buck. Who in the hell was this guy?

It wasn't everybody who'd kick their way into somebody else's 'domestic dispute,' walk into and out of the Towers without a scratch and then ask, bold as brass, to be taken to an address that was close enough to Richston Heights to give a girl a nosebleed.

Who the hell did this guy know at that end of the Harbor?

He wasn't saying, obviously. Still not quite tamed yet.

Still, she had to wonder. There wasn't much call for black muscle at that end. The swells usually imported their hard guys from somewhere with Nordic accents or, if they were slumming, from the local Ivans.

Max would stand out there as much or more than he did in the Downs. That couldn't be too healthy. The cops might not risk the lower depths too much these days, leaving the residents of that end of the Harbor mostly on their own, but they showed up like a lightning strike when *Whoever von Richbastard* hit 9-1-1.

Unlike the C Section, which could have done her serious ill had she been dumb enough to attempt a crossing, the worst she could expect in the heights was a roust.

If he knocked on the wrong door or shocked the wrong blue- haired blueblood, Max could actually disappear.

He had to know it and, since he seemed not to care, Layla's interest was on him like a newborn on a tit.

She was able to keep quiet until they crossed Beckman Way and the first green lawns and third stories began to appear on either side. Then she just had to ask.

"It's money, right?" He ignored her, another shock. "Come on. You're killing me here with the *I Love a Mystery* riff. You gotta give me something."

His head swiveled her way but, again, he kept mum. After a second he shook his head. Nope. Not spilling.

"That's rude, you know," she said aping a pout. "You're covering a lot of distance today, which you would have been doing on foot without me. You gotta be in on something big. So it's money or blood, right?"

"You don't need to know nothing about it," he said, eventually.

"Need?" she said. "No. This is strictly a want thing."

"Well, then," he said, turning back to his window. "You don't want to know nothing about it."

They didn't quite make it to the Heights; his address stopped them just short of the border, but it was close enough.

Since coming to the Harbor Layla had got near the Heights precisely once at a party some City Hall tweak threw for *Zapsoft* in a bid to get them to relocate to Gray Harbor.

They didn't, naturally, but the courting was as lavish as the city could produce, requiring tons of food, gallons of booze, confetti, Caesar Jones' Biggest Band and hot unattached girls from wall to wall.

Hostesses they called them and there was certainly no obligation to bed down with any of the guests. Layla hadn't felt any anyway.

She'd signed up for the quick cash and possible bonuses but, once she'd squeezed into the perfect black mini and set foot inside the cavernous main ballroom of Rollins House, she'd felt suddenly naked, exposed in the way you only were in nightmares about public humiliation.

Those weren't her people, that wasn't her place and, whatever her depth might be, she was well out of it there.

She'd spent the entire party in the rear courtyard chatting up the cadre of limo drivers who'd been left to cool their heels while their masters worked their dubious mojos on the human party favors inside.

She'd seen dawn upside down, lolling on the shiny black roof of an extra wide caddy swapping slugs from the bottle of Dom one of the drivers had snaked from inside. She had a memory of one chandelier and the silver doorknockers and it was more than she wanted.

328 Price wasn't a castle but it did s solid impression. Three stories, vaguely Victorian design with a burgundy and white color scheme that made Layla feel she could stroll up the little cobbled

GEOFFREY THORNE

walkway, knock on the door and be invited in for coffee. Nice.

Which made her nervous as hell. What was Max doing here? What possible business could he have in a place like this?

"You ain't gotta wait on me," he said when she put it to him. "This could take a while."

She reminded him she had nowhere to go and watched the frost fill up behind his dark brown eyes before he headed up to the house. It was true, for now anyway. There wasn't anywhere for her at the moment that was better than cooling her heels while he did whatever.

But, even if she had a pile of money waiting and Jumper, back from the dead, sprawled across it in nothing but his sunshine smile, knowing the end of Max's story was something she couldn't pass up.

Looks like you got a little hook in me too, she thought as she watched him ring the bell. *Have to do something about that.*

There was no answer so he moved around to the side of the house.

She was just trying to picture what sort of lives went on in these neighborhoods, behind the iron gates and wide tinted windows. She landed on something that was a cross between those weird family sitcoms from the 1970s and Little Women.

Hey, Mom! Whiskers ate the volcano I was making for science class! Don't worry, Timmy. I'll go along with you and explain the whole thing to Mr. Mortimer.

A part of her knew it couldn't be that way, that nothing in life was smooth or easy, no matter how rich or pretty you were, but another part, the largest one,

138

had to believe that money, enough money, could solve most of what ailed.

She mused about what she'd do with enough money, where she'd go, how she'd be, who, sucking down the fantasy like the smoke from her favorite brand of cigs.

She sat there on the hood of her car for all of ten minutes before somebody inside 328 Price started shooting.

"Chaohu, China. Hashima, Japan. Centralia, in Pennsylvania. Serjilla, Syria. Roanoke, in North Carolina. Adaminaby, Australia. Bodie, in California. Pripyat, ukraine. Ruddock, in Louisiana. Famagusta, Cyprus. Wagram, in Louisiana, again. Reschensee, Italy. Frenier, in Louisiana, again, still. I could go on and on. Maybe you don't know all of these names, these cities, these places. But I bet you know some. Know what they have in common? They're gone. That's right. Erased. Whether it was nature or whether it was man-madde isn't the point. They where here and now they're not. And we're deadly close to seeing this city going along after them. Please tell me I'm not the only one who sees this. Please tell me I'm not the only one willing to fight." – COUNCILMAN GERARD WOODMAN, MORNINGSTAR PRINT NEWS, AUGUST 10, 2011

TRACK 10: LA TORTURA

Okay, thought Max as the first bullet whizzed past his head to shatter its way through one of the ceramic tiles. The little splinters and chips jingled like wind chimes as they clattered into the metal sink below. *That one was on me.*

Muscle memory, something the medics said you got after a long time In Country doing the same shit over and over, kicked in as he upended the kitchen table and dived behind it for cover.

The second shot was interrupted by the top of the thick oak table. He felt the muffling thud ripple through it and into his shoulder, eating the bullet's momentum and saving his life the way his reflexes had the second before.

The thing was, he shouldn't have needed either his reflexes or his memory. Even before the desert he'd learned never to let somebody get the drop on him that way.

After that first harrowing month knocking in sandy doors and scanning every street for IEDs, keeping his personal radar dish active had jumped up from second nature to first.

This was his fault. He'd got lost drinking in the interior of the posh house, taking in the damned décor instead of scanning for threats and escape routes.

Looking at the beautiful mix of polished dark woods, perfectly subdued earth colors- different in every room- and the delicate little pieces of sculpture art from around the world, Max's mind had stuttered, trying to process how Reggie had scored a crib like this.

Even Lavall, for all his smarts and grit, was still chained to the C Section along with the rest. If this place belonged to Reggie, even a little, well, there was a long story coming for sure. Provided whoever it was that was trying to kill him ran out of bullets before they got their wish.

From the sound of the reports the shooter wasn't working with anything too big– maybe a .22 or a .38. It was nothing to write home about but still a hell of a lot more than he was packing which was nothing.

The table absorbed two more hits before he was sure it would keep eating the bullets for a little while longer. Nice craftsmanship there.

He took a couple of seconds to catch his breath and settle his mind. He'd been here before, after all. Shit, he'd been in worse more than once. He just had to suss it and mount the proper counter.

He could do this.

The Harbor was rough, sure, even lethal in places, but it wasn't like the desert. There were no screams, no sound of enormous metal gears grinding over ancient adobe mounds, no stink of shit and decay. There certainly wasn't any of that in this gingerbread house even with the gunplay.

The aroma of sawdust was everywhere, mixing with the pungent aerosol odor of gunpowder. Thin columns of sunlight cut across the space, making the tiny, flitty particles shine and dance. Time became amber around him as his mind ping-ponged back and forth between Then and Now.

The last time he'd almost lost his head this way-the literal, brains and blood blasted out like an instant Jackson Pollack way- had been that day he'd been on point, chasing insurgents through Fawazir.

Still a FNG, only two weeks into his tour and hopped up on adrenaline and lack of sleep he'd chased some Osama wannabe into one of those maybe-it's-a-house-maybe-a-viper-pit deals they laid out in rows over there.

He'd broken formation, ignored his corporal's orders to hang back in the din of shouting and gunfire and found himself alone in the dusty dark warren of stone and sand.

There had been this moment of absolute stillness and silence where he'd felt he could hear his blood moving in his head. They broke the moment with machetes and pistols.

After that there was a blur of stabs and punches and bullets screaming back and forth like alien mosquitoes from a scifi movie.

It was the second time in his life that he'd thought he really wasn't going to see the end of the next two minutes. He would have been right if that RPG hadn't taken out the wall and buried him and his killers in the ensuing rubble.

The Osamas were squashed mosquitoes after that and Max grew eyes in the sides and back of his head.

Those eyes kept him alive for the years of rotating in and out of the kill zones but, on setting foot back in the good old U.S., he was dumb enough to think he could let them go. Never again.

Damn it, he thought, casting around for something, anything, he could use to even things up between himself and the unseen shooter. There was nothing, just the overturned table still laying across the same grid of painted ochre clay that comprised the floor and the several rows of mahogany cabinets and drawers which, of course, he hadn't bothered to check to see where these folks kept the knives.

"Mother fuck," said a voice so low he couldn't decide if it was familiar or strange, male or female, young or old.

He heard something metal drop to the floor- the empty clip? Then there was the very faint pounding of footsteps retreating into the house. Somebody out there wanted to reload.

He was up and moving before he thought of it, back on the clock as the sergeant used to say.

He rejected the knives even as he noticed them standing in their little wooden block on the counter by the very nice Renaissance brand stove.

Knives locked you into having to do permanent damage to whoever you had to scrap and that wasn't where Max wanted to go.

He was the one trespassing, after all. It wouldn't be fair to dead somebody for protecting themselves and their home.

He opted instead for the heavy marble rolling pin that sat beside the knife block.

Better than a nightstick, he thought, following after the shooter.

There were two ways out of the kitchen- a door leading into the main part of the house and one that led off somewhere to the side.

Only one had the spent clip from a Baretta semi-auto lying across the threshold, so sideways it was.

.9mm, he thought, kicking it out of the way as he

went.

It must have been the smothering acoustics inside this place that had made him think .38. It was almost like the house had been soundproofed. He could barely hear his own footsteps as he passed through the shadowy rear hallway much less those of his attacker. Maybe it was the rugs and the wall hangings.

Jesus, he thought. *Who likes this crap?*

He'd never been a fan of the whole Back to Mother Africa thing where people who were born and raised in Buttfuck Georgia suddenly got it in their heads their great greats had come over in chains in some boat so now Michael Johnson who ran the liquor store on Beach and Wright was really Lebohang Mokose from the Sotho tribe.

These walls were covered with that damned kinte cloth pattern and the same fake "tribal" drawings you'd see hanging on the walls in one of those all-black sitcoms on TV.

"This is Gray Harbor, idiots," he always wanted to say. "Gray Harbor, U.S. of fucking A."

But, of course, he didn't. He was busy trying not to get killed while trespassing in the sitcom house.

There was a laundry room under what turned out to be a rear staircase and a door at the far end leading to the side yard- chained and bolted. He could see the thin layer of dust covering the lower stairs and he hadn't heard anyone going up so that left Door Number Three.

It was probably some kind of rec room or study or some other weird thing the almost-rich kept in joints like this.

The door was only half closed, affording him a

partial view of what looked like a closet door-shut- the edge of a large desk and, between them, a tall black floor lamp made to resemble a street light.

By now the shooter could have found that extra clip or even upgraded to something with more punch. All of a sudden the heavy rolling pin didn't seem like the friend it had ten seconds earlier. This wasn't the time to go in swinging.

He should have thought twice about opening that back door. And why the hell was it unlocked anyway? You'd think a place like this, with all that artsy crap all over, they'd lock the damn doors. He could just see a judge's face as he tried this explanation.

But, your honor, it was like they wanted somebody to come in. They left the door unlocked. The alarm system was down.

Yeah. Right. His best bet was to play this quiet and nice. Max could do nice when he had to.

"Hey, look," he said, his voice sounding strangely hoarse, almost artificial in the unnatural stillness of the place. "I ain't looking for trouble here. This is just a mistake."

He edged closer to the doorway, trying to find and track any movement from the other side. The hint of a shadow could be the difference between life and death right now.

"I ain't here to boost nothing and I ain't out to hurt you. I'm just trying to touch up with somebody I know s'posed to be cribbing here. Reggie Waters okay? Maybe you know-"

He heard the hammer click behind him and spun, bringing the rolling pin up in front of his face in an instinctive block.

Muscle memory again. Damn.

The shooter was like a god damned ninja or something. That laundry room had looked totally empty when he went past.

Idiot!

The shot went off a split-second after, exploding the pin in Max's hand, sending bits of jagged marble flying everywhere.

It staggered him but the shooter, instead of finishing him off, shrieked and attacked him with teeth and nails and about a hundred and fifteen bounds of body weight pressing and kicking and gouging at him anyway it could. What the hell?

He fell backwards, trying at once to fend off the frenzied shooter and to keep his balance and failing at both.

He hit the floor with a muffled thud, his attacker's full weight riding him down and the hurricane of bites and slashes to his face preventing him from even getting a clear look.

It felt like a chick from the weight and the thing with the biting but he'd been on the wrong side of too many crackheads too may times to make assumptions.

Fingers and thumbs jabbed at his eyes; the teeth tried to tear into his cheeks; the knees pistoned attacks at his crotch over and over and all he could do was try to fend them off without really doing damage of his own.

Why couldn't he learn this lesson? Every time he crossed the line there was an ocean of shit on the other side.

"Okay," he said, trying to slide his words in between the shrieks and bites. "Okay, chill. I told you,

149

I ain't–"

He took a shot to the groin that ended the conversation even as the chick- it was obviously a chick now; he could smell her and feel her skin- raked her nails across his eyes.

He shoved her away, hard, and pressed one forearm into his face in an attempt to squeeze out the pain. He heard her thump against the floor and skid into the far wall and, just as he was wondering what happened to her gun, she was back with it, straddling his chest with the muzzle pressed against his forehead.

Max froze and emptied his mind. He tried not to think about the hundreds, maybe thousands of times somebody somewhere had tried to end him this way. Skilled professionals with training and equipment hadn't managed to put him down.

That army of Dogs couldn't do it but here he was, about to get aired out by super ninja babysitter on the Huxtables' kitchen floor.

"Okay, honey," said a familiar voice. "That's about enough of that. Let's everybody calm down, okay?"

He felt the woman go still, her ass settling back into his chest as her thighs clenched against him. The gun pulled back and he let his arm fall away from his eyes, wincing every time a little light peaked through the lids.

"Hey," said Layla smiling down at him over the woman's shoulder. At least it looked and sounded like Layla.

"Hey," he said, elbowing himself up to a seated position.

His eyes still stung too much to keep them open for more than a blink. Pulling himself up and navigating his way to the sink was like crossing a dance club with the lights on full strobe.

He managed not to crash into the table on the way to the stainless steel oasis and was as grateful for the cold water that erupted from the tap as any Bedouin stumbling out of the Sahara.

"Just gimme a second," he said, letting the water do its soothing work.

"Take your time," she said. "I just need to get the steel off your girlfriend here and we're good."

His eyes cleared in time to see the handoff and to be not quite as surprised as he would have thought at the identity of his attempted murderer. He knew that face and figure almost as well as he knew his own.

"Come on, Sis," said Layla, reaching around. "Let's have it."

"I ain't your sister, bitch," said the other. But she passed the gun back. If looks could kill the murder in her eyes would have sent both Max and Layla up in an explosion of flames.

"And we can watch the language too," said Layla.

"Fuck you."

"Wow," said Layla. "Somebody's got a mouth on her anyway."

That was no joke. Max knew their little shit talker could let loose a hell of a lot more in the way of vicious invective when she felt free.

He stared at her, unblinking, the way he might stare at the spirit of his dead grandmother or a talking dog. She actually did have a little ninja thing going on with the black sweats and hoodie.

Yeah, the years had softened her up a little and she had her hair permed into something shoulder long and white-girl straight but it was her. Just like the old days. Even with her face tilted away from him and half of her perm hanging over the left side he would know her anywhere.

The reception she gave him was no mystery and he had no doubt she'd have ventilated him good if she'd been able.

"Thanks," said Layla, cheerfully exchanging the Baretta for her own weapon. When Max saw why, he smiled and shook his head.

The "gun" Layla had pressed into her neck was just the business end of a tire iron. Jesus. That bit was so old it had lost its hair but, obviously, not its teeth.

"Damn, girl," he said, splashing more water into his cuts and wincing.

"Hey," said Layla. "You work with what you got."

Once the Baretta was safely in one of her hands she set the tire iron down on the counter, eliciting an angry "You gotta be shitting me," from her charge. Layla winked at her and blew her a little smooch but the gun stayed level.

Max winced as the water got into one particularly deep gash on his face and then reached for a dish towel.

"Cops are coming," said the girl in black.

Max shook his head. "You don't want the cops here or they'd be here already."

"Fuck you, Max," she said. "Fuck you and this white bitch."

"Hey!" said Layla, looking hurt. "Why do I have to be a bitch?"

"Ask your mother," said the girl in black. "Bitch."

"Yeah, this one's a charmer," said Layla. "Please

tell me you got what you came for."

"You ain't getting shit off me," said the girl in black. "Y'all lucky you still breathing."

"I feel lucky," said Layla and shot the can-we-go look at Max. Max ignored her. He did what he could with the water and batted his face dry, leaving tiny splotches of watery blood on the flower pattern. His attention was entirely on the woman in black.

"The fuck you looking at?" she said through her teeth. It was obvious that the Baretta was the only thing keeping her from having another go at Max's face.

He could almost see the rage rippling under her ebony skin like a nest of cobras pining to strike. Same as always. Same as before. The years hadn't changed her a bit.

Except... except...

The way she kept her head a little bit bowed and tilted just to the left, away from him- that was new. At first Max had thought it was just to make her glare that much more feral as it burned out from beneath her artificial bangs; now he thought something else.

The hair was too well-placed, too much a part of her overall symmetry to be a coincidence. She'd always been like that: particular about her image.

Even at her lowest, even when she was on the pipe she had somehow managed to maintain her picture of cocoa butter sexuality that drew the boys like honey bees. Max was no different.

"You wanna see it?" said the girl in black, almost snarling. "Is that it? You came all this way back here to get a look at what you done?"

"Came to settle up, is all," said Max. "You

shouldn't have tried to keep that to yourself."

"Settle up?" she said, hysteria creeping into her voice where there had only been anger before. "You think you can just come back and put it all right like that? You think it's easy like that? You think I'm just gonna let you-"

"Yeah," said Max, his own voice dropping into something much closer to a growl than he liked to admit. "Damned right, you gonna let me. I got a right to-"

"You got a right to shit," she said, almost screamed actually. It was enough to force Layla to remind her who had the gun.

The girl in the black sweats shot her a look that said it might just be worth testing Layla's resolve if it meant she could gouge some more bits out of Max's flesh. It passed.

"You got nothing. You got what you did to me, Max. You got that and nothing else. You want to talk about rights and settling up, you better settle up with me off the top."

"What I did to you?" said Max, moving within fist's reach of her. It was clear that whatever it was that had been seething in the girl in black had somehow infected Max also. "I saved your ass. I pulled you out."

A stream of *fuck you's* and *motherfuckers,* like M-16 bullets, ripped out of her, peppering Max, obliterating anything he might say in his defense.

"You pulled me out? You pulled me out? Who put me in, motherfucker? Who did this?"

Before Layla could move, the girl shoved away from her, shaking her long black tresses so violently

154

that they whipped about her face like streamers caught in a cyclone.

When they settled, when she was still again, her entire face was on display.

"Jesus," said Layla, backing away slightly and letting the Baretta dip a bit too low. "Jesus H. Christ."

The scar covered nearly half of the other woman's face, distorting her otherwise catlike features into something that looked both hideous and pitiable at once.

It was as if the flesh on that side of her face- and her neck, the scar ran below the collar of her hoodie- had been dripped and smudged across her muscles like hot wax.

The eyebrow was intact, still doubling the arch of its twin even as the glaring amber eye was equally undamaged but the flesh-

It took Max less time to recover from the shock than Layla- a full twenty seconds- so he was ready when the girl snatched the Baretta back and tried to aim it at his face.

His hand caught hers, forcing them up at exactly the wrong angle to do damage. She got the shot off, there was no way she wouldn't, but the bullet clanged against the hanging metal lamp and buried itself in the ceiling.

Max tore the gun from her hand with his right and tossed it back to Layla who popped out the clip and racked the last bullet from the pipe.

With his left hand Max took hold of both of the woman's wrists, crushing them together so hard she forgot her anger just long enough to gasp. He yanked her forward, holding her fast despite her violent attempts to pull free. She wrenched her arms twice before accepting it as hopeless.

"This don't mean shit," she said. "You just as fucked now as you was when you came up in here."

"Just let me talk to him," said Max still in that tone that was at once like pleading and like a threat. "Just let me-"

"Ten K," she said. "What?"

"The docs say it'll cost a hundred thousand to put me back like I was," she said. "Insurance covers half. My man put together forty. I need ten more or I can't do it."

"Ten thousand dollars."

"You heard me, nigga," said the woman. Her voice was calm. She had begun to smile, showing her perfect white predator's teeth. "You want to see him. You want to 'settle up,' you bring my money. Then we talk."

"You can't do that."

"It's done," she said. "Try to test me, nigga. You think you got anything that's gonna hurt me worse than this?"

She obviously meant the scar and, though he wanted nothing more than to squeeze her hands until they snapped, until she gave him what he wanted, what he'd come all this way for, he knew it wouldn't change anything.

She wouldn't budge; he could see steel in her eyes under the honey color. She would have him murdered before he got ten steps towards his goal if he crossed her. One call to the right people and he wouldn't leave enough behind to make a ghost.

Some of the steam went out of him then. He let her

hands go, barely watching as she rubbed first one wrist and then the other to get the feeling back.

Layla flashed him a questioning look but he just gave her one quick headshake in response. It was done now, all done.

"Come on," he said, forcing himself to take the ten steps out of the kitchen and into the back yard. "Let's go."

•••

"What the hell was that?" she asked him when they were back on the curb by her car. He was halfway gone to that faraway place he kept inside.

"Nothing," he said. "Just... nothing."

"'Nothing' my ass," she said. "That was some deep biblical shit going on in there. End of the world shit."

"If you say so."

"Well," she said, sliding in and opening the door for him. He moved slowly, on autopilot, as if he needed her to say things to him to keep him in the world. "Shit. You want to get some lunch or something?"

"What?" he said.

He was obviously distracted, thinking and, damn it, not sharing. Again.

"Lunch, man," she said. "No way in hell I let this go without getting the news on what the fuck just happened in there."

"Yeah," he said. "Sure. Whatever."

"Who the hell was that chick?" said Layla as he slid into the passenger's side.

"That?" said Max, wistfully, not necessarily talking to her. "That was Reggie."

Premiere: October 10, 2014 Showtime: 5 PM

Attire: 1990s Ghetto Fab

PLEASE come on down to ALPHABET STREET for an evening of DIAMONDS & PEARLS as we SET IT OFF for the Fifteen Year CLASS REUNION TO END CLASS REUNIONS.

Saturday, October eighteenth two thousand eighteen at five o'clock in the evening Gray Harbor Inn, GRAY HARBOR

Hosted by: Your Reunion Committee – **Mass Evite to Graduates of Medgar Evers High School, Class of 1998**

TRACK 11: USE ME

The clouds opened up again about the time they headed back towards the Downs. The wet never really cleaned anything, only made rivers out of the streets and gutters, filling them with the crap that normally coated every wall.

But she was happy to be back in more familiar warrens where at least she knew what boogies hid under what beds.

He grunted something that sounded like "yeah" when she mentioned food. At least that's what she wanted to hear. He was off in his head again, just like before, wandering.

He was a deep well, all right, but he could definitely handle himself. Anybody seeing the way he held back with Mrs. Housefire would know the only thing gumming his works was he didn't want to hit a chick.

It was another of his tells; he was sentimental.

The realization shocked her because, so far, he hadn't seemed anywhere near that much of a rube.

The Harbor didn't treat soft feelings well and it kicked the living shit out of anybody stupid enough to hold onto them for longer than the time it took to get a good laugh at the idea.

You could afford that kind of weakness in other places; at least she supposed you could. Places out of books she'd read, places where the glossy fashion mags sent the stick girls to hold up their clothes while somebody snapped their pics- those places, maybe, you could afford to be soft or stupid or slow. Not Gray Harbor. She couldn't count the number of guys she knew of who'd been sent to the morgue over pissing off or pissing on the wrong chick.

Weaker sex, my lily white ass, she'd thought more than once. *Like a girl can't shoot you or put an ice pick though your eye.*

That old-school chivalry added up to a big stack of disrespect in her book though she wasn't above using that moronic POV against those who still held it, she didn't have to like the experience.

She didn't.

She didn't like what it said about what the boys were thinking and she didn't like what it said about her for letting them think it, even if she got something shiny out of the exchange.

All of a sudden Layla wasn't sold that Max was what she wanted, what she needed just now and, just now, it was desperately necessary for her to be sold.

"You know *Mickey Six's?*" she said to him as they crossed DuBois, leaving the Heights behind for good. He didn't know the place but he obviously didn't care.

His mind was on "Reggie" and whatever it was that bound them and a meal was a meal was a meal.

There were five *Mickey Six's* in the Harbor, the little chain doing its best to compete with the bigger, multi-state eateries whose style it didn't quite ape. Mickey himself was some kind of local hero, a sort of half Robin Hood-Half Dillinger who'd blown through town in the 1930s and cut himself a bit a of a swath.

Layla liked their vanilla malts and the big retro style movie posters that adorned the walls, depicting the original Mickey as the lead in films he'd never starred in because they'd never been made.

She liked Mickey's swarthy good looks too though she would've laid odds that the real article was a sight less easy on the eyes than the Hollywood polish. Hard guys always were.

Watching Max murder his second stack of Mickey's Hard Six– buckwheat flapjacks that actually did manage to taste home made– Layla wondered what ol' Mickey would have thought of the big guy.

The thirties being what they were, probably not much. A man like Max would have been dead or in prison PDQ in those days. He was just too much his own guy for all that Jim Crow crap.

Easy sister, she told herself. *Don't like the sonuvabitch too much. You need him.*

"All right," she said after he'd wolfed down his eighth flapjack and chased it with another gulp each of coffee and milk. "Let's have it."

"Hm?" he said, reaching for the syrup. "What."

"You think you're gonna sit there, chowing, and not tell what the hell that was all about?" she said, snatching the little jug away before he could touch it.

"Quit playing," he said, giving her the no-nonsense look. She held the thing high, dangling it like a carnival prize.

"Nope," she said. "Spill."

His features hardened again a bit but, she noted with pleasure, not nearly all the way. She was getting in.

"What did I tell you about treating me like a mark?" he said.

"Um, don't?"

"Well, then?" He reached for the syrup again and,

163

again, she held it just out of range.

"Nope," she said. "Spill."

"Why you always pressing?" he said.

He gave up on the prize, opting instead to take a few bricks out of the mountain of butter pads he'd built.

"Just making conversation," she said. She wrinkled her lips into a pout meant just for him and set the syrup down on her lap. "I mean if you want me walking out of here thinking you're the one put a torch to Mrs. Housefire back there, that's your trip. But, like, really. There's no way, right? That was just bullshit. Right?"

He made a show of ignoring her in favor of the butter pads, methodically unfolding three in deliberate succession and smearing each in some arcane pattern across the pancakes' freckled skin.

Layla stood it for about ten seconds before she opened the dam.

"Aw, come on," she said, swiping the remains of Mt. Margarine off the table. Blanking the waitress's raised eyebrows– *ask the boss for hazard pay, honey*– she leaned across her empty plates until she was near enough to press her lips to his forehead. "I didn't walk in right when I did, that chick would have aired you out good. From where I'm sitting that means you owe me."

"Yeah?" said Max, ignoring her closeness.

"Hell, yeah," she said, slumping back into her seat. "Lucky for you I just want the goods on all that. So, spill, dude. Fair is fair."

He took five solid minutes to finish off his hotcakes. She watched as he labored over each bite, chewing so slowly, so deliberately that there was just no way it could be accidental.

He was playing with her, the impenetrable bastard; he was actually trying to irritate her and it was working.

Even as she stifled the urge to reach out and pop him one across the nose she allowed herself a secret little grin. He was playing with her– another sign, despite appearances, that she'd gotten in.

He chewed the last of his last bite, swallowed it, took a hard swig of his OJ, killing the last of that, and let out a low thin rumble– his version of a sigh.

"Okay," he said.

"Okay?" she said.

"Yeah."

"Goody."

Watching her the way a guard dog watches the property line, Max reached into the folds of his jacket and pulled out a bit of something– paper, folded small and tight– and passed it too her. The way his fingers didn't quite release the thing at first, lingering just a little too long before handing it off to a new set of digits, told her that this was something important.

Don't smile, she thought, but she wanted to. This was another sign that she had gotten in, after all, and in was where she wanted to be.

She watched him back; her eyes locked with his as she unfolded the thing, letting him see how deliberately her fingers worked the paper, how seriously she was taking this for him.

That's right, big boy, her eyes seemed to say. *I'm on your side. We're friends.*

It was smooth, covered in plastic or... tape! He'd

165

protected the thing with a couple layers of clear sticking tape, poor man's lamination.

When it was open on the table in front of her she saw it was an old front page from *The Runner*, Gray Harbor's big newspaper.

The headline- NEIGHBORHOOD CRACK CASTLES STYMIE POLICE EFFORTS- meant no more to her than the over- exposed photo of a row of brownstones in the Section they'd put below.

She was just looking up to ask what the hell this was supposed to be when she saw he had another bit of paper in his hand, also covered in plastic tape and folded into an eighth of itself. It also had meaning for him, she could see that on his face.

She took it, just as reverently as she had the other and, just as delicately unfolded it as well.

This was just a bit of printer paper with words typed on them. Something he'd done himself?

"We are not enemies, but friends," she read softly, mouthing the words like soft familiar chocolates. "We must not be enemies.

Though passion may have strained, it must not break our bonds of affection. The mystic chords of memory, stretching from every battlefield and patriot grave to every living heart and hearthstone all over this broad land, will yet swell the chorus of the Union, when again touched, as surely they will be, by the better angels of our nature."

They had meaning for him, she could see that, even without knowing why he thought they needed to be kept and carried with him at all times.

She looked up again, clearly lost, clearly unable to connect the words to the newspaper to Reggie to Max.

"I don't," she said and stopped. The words tapped something inside her, making it ring like a tiny silver bell at the bottom of a deep chasm. The unknown something was familiar too, in a way she didn't like. "I don't get it."

He had another bit of folded paper in his hand, easily pegged as another newspaper page. She frowned. There was something about the way he was looking at her, the way the words rattled around inside her, something that made her skin feel tight and cold.

"Dude," she said. "What is this?"

"Just read it," he said. His voice was so quiet, almost murmuring. The way his eyes were on her, like he was looking right through her pupils, straight to the back of her skull, had her reaching for the last page without thinking.

ARSON SUSPECTED IN TENAMENT FIRE, the headline read and, below it, another photo, nearly identical to the first except for flames ripping out of the windows and across the roofs.

"I don't get it," she said, finally.

"You don't get it," he said.

"Crack house," she said, rereading, her eyes flitting back and forth between the pages. "Burned up crack house. So what?"

"So," he intoned, still staring. "What."

Her eyes went back to the pages, her brain back to scanning, processing.

Think, stupid, she told herself. *Think.*

It took her a second to suss out that the second row of houses was the same as the first. As revelations went it was not particularly helpful. She read a little of the first article finding the same old phrases– the police control things during the day but, after dark, DuBois Boulevard belongs to the runners and the dealers who own them- then she moved on to the second where another sentence leaped out.

... when asked for comment about the damage caused by the fire, which included injury to six apparently homeless squatters, the sentiment was decidedly positive.

"Good riddance," said one elderly resident who refused to give her name.

"Somebody should have burned them bastards out last year ."

Layla's mind raced. What the hell did Max have to do with this? Why was he carrying this crap around with him, wrapped up clean and tight, protected from rain and decay?

Stuff like this was always happening in the Harbor, especially in the Section. It was obvious that Mrs. Housefire was one of the squatters but Max didn't look like he'd got burned.

She blamed him for it though. She blamed him enough to go full-on lethal at the sight of him.

"Oh, come on," she said as her brain finally put the bits together. "No way."

"What?" he said.

"You did this?" she said, scarcely believing it, even as she said the words. He nodded. "You? Captain Frigging America?"

"I ain't no Captain America," he said.

"Well," she said, her attention now split between the queer expression on his face– not quite sad, not quite cold– and the newspapers. "Now I really gotta hear this."

"That's it," he said. "You got it."

"This?" she said, pushing the pages back towards him. "This ain't nothing. Just words and pictures."

"Well," he said. "What you want?"

"The juice, man," she said. "The skinny. That chick, Reggie, she was in there, yeah?"

"Yeah. She was in there."

"So, what," said Layla. "You didn't know?"

"I knew where she was," he said, carefully folding the first page in half, then in quarter, before sliding it back into his jacket. "I'm the one pulled her out."

"Well, she looked grateful as hell to me."

Max ignored her, taking the second article, folding it and replacing it like the first.

Watching him put her suddenly in mind of one of the few times she'd ever been to church. She'd snuck in once just to get some peace from her mom's crazy boyfriend, a man who was all hands and hot breath on her six-year old skin.

Sitting quiet and unseen in the rear of the place, she watched in a sort of rapture watching as the alter boys wiped down the giant candlesticks that framed the podium there.

It was clear to her this was a duty they'd done many times and would do many times again. It was clear that they neither loved nor hated the job but did it, she felt even then, because it was what they were meant to do.

Max is like those boys, she thought and relaxed again as the new piece of his puzzle fell into place.

"How come you burned the place down," she said.

For the first time since she'd met him, since she'd first seen him at the diner, Max's face went soft. For just a moment he stopped being the giant granite homicide machine she'd prayed for and became the one thing she had the least use for just now: a man.

"Had enough, I guess," he said softly.

He was back there, she could see it, reliving it, feeling it all again. "I lived across from them fuckers for a whole year. Seen 'em doing business, scrapping, pissing in the street. Seen the teenage girls getting turned out for a taste of that shit. Boys too. And moms and dads. I seen all that for all that time and I thought, 'somebody gotta do something.'"

"Yeah, okay, maybe," she said. "But why you?"

"Why not me," was his answer. "Wasn't nobody else doing shit. Wasn't nobody else gonna."

It was so simple the way he said it, like that's just what anybody would do in his place. For a second everything smart or crafty or savvy about Layla went away and she was just staring at him, blatantly, as if his face had peeled suddenly away to reveal one of those aliens from the movies.

She would have preferred a monster, she thought. She understood monsters; she knew how they ticked, what they ate, what they wanted.

She'd been around monsters of one sort or another for her whole life, long enough to be wary and to always keep her eyes open but never to be scared of them.

Max scared her. Suddenly and right to the bone he scared her cold.

For the first time since their partnership had begun, she thought she understood him and, understanding, she began to think that he really wasn't the right guy for what she needed.

"So, then what?" she said in her smallest voice. "You just split?"

"Marines," he said.

"Smart," she said, meaning it. "Good way to keep the cops off you."

"Wasn't worried about no cops."

"Dealers, then," she said, after a little thought. "I mean I'd get my ass out of Dodge too. They don't like when you fuck with their money."

Max said nothing but his face had gone halfway hard again.

"So, okay," she went on, still noodling it. "So you fucked off out of the Harbor. You got away with it and you never caught a bullet."

"Not so far," he said, almost completely stone again.

"So, what'd you come back for?" she said.

"My son," he said. "*Our* son. Terrance."

"You and Mrs. Housefire? No way."

"Boy needs a father," he said, again like that was all there was to it.

She had questions. She had miles of them stacking up inside her like the worst rush-hour tangle in history.

Somehow they wouldn't come.

Something in her, the vestiges of that little silver tone maybe, kept her mouth still and her mind whirling.

Max wasn't the guy.

He looked like the guy. He even seemed like the guy when he was pissed off and deadly but, now that she could really see what he was, she knew that he, maybe more than any other guy in the Harbor, was absolutely not what she needed.

She had to think now. She had to think fast and she had to think smart. She couldn't do it with him sitting there all Good and Solid and looking at her that way.

"Hitting the ladies'," she said, rising. She placed the syrup on the table where it belonged. "Don't ghost on me, yeah?"

He grunted something, fully stone again now, and beckoned for the waitress.

•••

The alley stank, the uncovered dumpsters spewing odorous clouds of decaying breakfast waffle mixed with the vestiges of too many shmears of sour cream.

For the ten millionth time since she'd done it, she lamented her decision to give up nicotine.

Girl could kill for a smoke, she thought.

Why the hell did she press Max for his God damned life story? Why couldn't she leave him mysterious and dangerous and perfect? Why did she have to be so god damned smart?

Things were falling apart again and this time there was no net waiting to catch her when they finally did collapse.

Snap it up, Layla, she thought. *Work it out.* But, without the helpful bone and its gentle caress of smoke, her mind was locked and motionless.

"Jesus Christ," said a familiar voice from the hidden side of the nearest dumpster. "What the fuck is taking so long?"

Perfect, she thought when Nicky stepped into view. *Just fucking perfect.*

JOHN FRANKEL: But you've got to admit, the OCCUPY movement seems largely minority free. Your art has always been political in nature, why not lend your name and talents to this?

DARIUS HALL JR: (LAUGHS) You're serious. Wow. Okay. Real answer. This is just me, talking, of course. What's happened to the country is that everybody else is starting– just starting, mind you– to get a taste of being treated the way we blacks always have been and they're scared.

I was talking with a friend of mine about the massive joblessness and how so many companies are laying off long-term employees in favor of short term contractors. This saves the company a stack of money in health care costs and it makes everyone's status less secure. No possibility of seniority so no dug-in employee pushback when some suit at the top wants a change.

Most Americans aren't used to that. People are also not used to having their civil liberties restricted and their voices going unheard. But we are. Black people. Latins, to some degree. Natives, for sure. That's been our history here so I can easily see why most Blacks don't care one way or the other about OCCUPY. It's not about us. This is a bunch of people who thought they were part of the privileged class finding out that they're not. Sure, they're unhappy about the news of where they actually sit in this society. Welcome to not being white in America." – **From ART TALK:360, November 5th, 2011**

TRACK 12: FACE DOWN

All day. All God damned day, from the time the stupid slut twisted the big gorilla into taking a ride, through what Nicky thought should have been a suicidal trip to the Section all the way up to the border of the Heights and down again to this greasy excuse for a *Mickey Six's,* he had shadowed her because that was the fucking plan.

Well, getting monkey boy into her car, leading him to a place where he'd take a short nap in Nicky's trunk before taking a permanent one in the dirt outside a particular warehouse he'd picked out, that was the plan. Part of.

This was the plan twisting. This was the plan maybe going to hell.

All those detours must have been Layla's idea of a joke. Or maybe she was too stupid to keep more than one fucking notion in that airy box of sex positions she called a skull.

Whatever.

Her ass would take a few smacks from his belt for that later, once all this was finished. In the meantime Nicky had a few questions, a few reminders and a few minutes to pass them on to her.

Stanis was still out there, damn it. No matter what he said about waiting 'til evening, Nicky knew that Stanis could change his mind on a fucking dime. Or he could have been lying to begin with, just letting Nicky twist for a while before unhooking Gregor's leash.

Nicky's hand was already in her hair, holding,

twisting, yanking her close to him so he could make his points to her face.

"Hey!" she yelped, her voice taking on the half-angry, half- apologetic lilt he loved. He always forgot of sexy she was when he was hurting her and always took pleasure when she reminded him this way. "Let go!"

"Maybe you didn't hear me," he said, pulling her face close to his and watching her go from squint to glare as he yanked hard at her roots. "I said, 'What. Is. Taking. So. Fucking. Long?'"

He punctuated his words with a sharp tugs, each eliciting these feeble little squeaks from her that had him thinking of her on her back somewhere, sweating up some sheets. Jesus, she was hot. The image pulled him away for a second so he didn't quite hear her mumbled response.

"What?" he said, yanking. "What's that?"

"Sorry," she said, all breathy and low. She knew what she was doing, damn her. And it was working all right but he didn't have time for foreplay. This was serious.

"Sorry, my ass," he said. "I told you, this has to be done by dark. You and monkey boy are burning daylight like that crazy Russian isn't out there waiting to gut me like a goddamn fish."

"Hey," she said, finally pulling away from him and leaving a few blond wisps behind in his palm for her trouble. "You think it's so easy to work this guy, be my fucking guest."

Wow. Spunky. That was new. Nicky couldn't make up his mind if he liked it or if it was cause for more licks from his belt. Something to mull.

176

He slapped her.

"Who the fuck do you think you're talking to?" he said.

Her eyes went dewy again and her posture returned to the familiar one, the one he'd trained her to adopt whenever he was around. Eyes mostly down, voice low and respectful, just a little bit of fear tensing up her shoulders.

"I'm sorry, okay," she said. "Baby, this guy, I don't know, he's like crazy or something. I'm not sure he's the right–"

His hand whipped out again, catching her jacket collar and yanking her back to him. Holding her close and tight, he pulled the knife out of his jacket pocket and put the blade flat on her cheek. She trembled a bit at the touch.

"I don't care if he's Charles Fucking Manson," he whispered in her ear. "We don't work this out the way I told you, before sunset, Stanis is gonna put this fucking knife in my fucking neck."

He yanked her back, hard, one final time before slamming her to the ground. She went down like a rag doll, riding out his anger like she always did, but getting the point as well.

Things had gone as far south as Nicky was willing to let them. There was one way to handle tough guys and it was to be the smartest one in the room.

If he was going to skate out of this with his blood in his body and his skin still wrapping it tight, the plan had to work the way he said.

And Layla needed to hold up her fucking end.

"Now you do like I told you," he said, crouching down beside her, his voice buzzing in her ear like a lover's whisper. "You get that monkey juiced up and where he needs to be, P D fucking Q, or I'm gonna finish the job I started on you last night."

He straightened up again and did a quick scan of the alley, making sure they were still alone. His jacket needed smoothing so he did that.

He sniffed, momentarily distracted by the stench of rotting food and piss and whatever else got crushed into the grimy brick and concrete.

Fucking disgusting. It was a couple of long moments before he remembered she was still there at his feet, mumbling something to herself.

"Huh?" he said. "What's that?"

One time, when Stanis had told him to shadow Gregor for a bit so he could learn about the relationship between actions and consequences, Nicky had watched the big psycho get into a scrap with some of Vig Haardt's boys.

Vig was like Stanis only Swedish or Norwegian or something. He had his own crew, his own territory and he maintained a sort of a truce with the Ivans twelve days out of twenty.

The other eight days was straight-up war. The week Nicky shadowed him Gregor's job was to deliver a message from Stanis to Vig.

Somebody owed somebody something or there was a dispute about a card game or a girl or whatever but Vig wasn't about to take any shit off of Gregor even if it was ultimately coming from Stanis.

So Gregor laid into him and his boys in the back room of that squalid little gas station they used to front Vig's chop shop.

It was fists at first, mainly because Gregor wasn't

there to kill anybody but, when one of Vig's boys pulled a hammer and started swinging, Gregor went to Plan B.

Nicky had just stood back, rooted by the front door, as Gregor pounded those three men to death, cut them to bits, shoved them into garbage bags and carried them out to the trunk of his car.

Gregor never spoke to him, never acknowledged he was even present until, after he'd doused the place with gasoline and lit it up, he looked Nicky square in the face and said, "Come on."

Though watching Gregor in action had turned Nicky's blood to water and had him fighting to maintain control of his bladder, the look in those eyes had been worse. It wasn't just winter in there; it was the fucking Ice Age.

It was the first time he'd seen eyes like that and he'd thought it was the last until Layla looked up at him from the gutter.

"Next time," she said in a low even tone that spoke of something like the snow inside Gregor. "Next time you put your hands on me, I'm gonna kill you."

Maybe she meant it. Maybe, in some other time and place where she wasn't just one more neighborhood twist and he wasn't the guy who was going to outsmart the Ivans and skate with a hundred K in invisible drug money (not to mention the drugs themselves), she might have been able to pull it off.

Too bad for her this wasn't that time or that place and, as long as she did what the fuck he told her, exactly the way he told her, he would always be the smart guy.

He laughed in her face and kissed her angry lips.

"You know you love it," he said.

He was up then, moving away from her, out of the alley, away from the stench, already thinking about the future.

"You need to blow him or something to keep him happy, that's cool," he said over his shoulder. "Just don't fuck him. Gotta draw the line somewhere."

Then he was gone, never looking back to see her up on her feet again and on her way inside to do as she was told.

GAME THEORY is a method for analyzing circumstances where a person's success is based upon the choices of others. It is has applications in economics, political science, psychology, logic and biology among other disciplines. It was first concerned with zero sum games, where one person's gains precisely equal the losses of another. Since then Game Theory has become a blanket description of anything in science that is concerned with logic and outcomes involving choice. - From Webisaurus, a free internet encyclopedia

TRACK 13: I AGAINST I

No.

It took her a few seconds longer than she wanted to pull herself back to composure.

The door to her little white room had swung wide open and she had some difficulty wrestling down the urge to bolt inside.

The pages of *The Prince* flapped gently in some unseen breeze, beckoning like a pair of pursed lips.

No.

There wasn't anything there for her, not just now. The book had no more secrets anyway. It galled her to have slipped so much in front of Nicky but he'd actually managed to surprise her, showing up like that.

No.

She could still feel the anger, long suppressed, long controlled and channeled into better things, rippling under her skin, wanting out.

She was suddenly remembering the first time his hands were on her that way.

It wasn't a picture so much as it was a feeling– his fingers pressing into her bicep, bruising her instantly and giving her that perfect feeling of understanding Nicky completely, loathing him utterly and knowing that he, more than any previous horse, was one she could ride to the finish.

No.

She had to get back on the program, hers, his, whatever. Things still had to be done, dominos knocked over and, even though he was just a twitchy, abusive fuck, Nicky was right; everything needed to be wrapped up by dark.

The wreck of their meal had been cleared away by the time she returned to him, replaced by a copy of the *Free Harbor* that he had open to the jobs section.

He barely noticed as she slid into her seat, the various want ads occupying all his attention. He was made of stone again; she could tell from the flatness behind his eyes.

So she waited a bit, burning minutes she didn't really have, hoping he would open his door again.

"So anyway," she said when it became clear he saw more in his paper than in her. "The way I figure it is; I need somebody to watch my ass 'til I can get my shit and get out of Dodge."

"Figured that out by yourself," he said, not looking up.

"And you need somebody to hook you up with some kinda serious cash to get you square with Mrs. Housefire," she went on, unperturbed. "And, y'know, your kid."

"That's my business," he said, still non-committal.

He had a pen out and was making little checks beside the ads that took his interest.

"Sure," she said. "But what I was thinking is-"

"Thinking again, huh?" he said. "Not you."

She couldn't tell if the sarcasm was for fun or for digging at her so she ignored it.

"So, what I was thinking is, you stick with me while I run this errand-"

"Errand?"

"If I'm getting out of here I need to get my stuff."

He mumbled something and she was pretty sure she saw a smile trying to curl the edge of his mouth. "You watch my back while I do this and I can give you that ten K you need for your boy."

He shot her another of his brick and mortar looks, just a quick one, before folding the paper and rising to his feet. He tossed a few crumpled bills on the table and headed for the door.

As he passed through the doors he tossed most of the paper into the trash bin, only holding the JOBS section in one massive brown hand.

She caught up to him again on the street when he paused for a second, obviously trying to decide which way to go.

"Why are you always walking away from me when I'm talking to you?" she said.

"'Cause you're full of shit," he said.

She could feel the color in her cheeks and knew her blush was visible to him. He'd stung her with that; she was full of shit, but he didn't know why. She could build on that if she had time.

There was a cabstand across the street and he was already in motion towards it, forcing her to chase him again. The sign said there'd be another taxi in fifteen minutes.

"Come on," she said, getting close, talking low. "I'm serious here."

"You got ten thousand bucks," he said, making a real show of not looking directly at her.

He was acting like she was one of those Greek myth things she'd read in school. What were they called? They turned people to stone by looking at them, she remembered. It would have been funny if it wasn't so insulting. Why be scared of getting turned to stone when you're already made of it?

She would have told him just that except she suddenly realized what it meant: he was scared of her. Maybe she hadn't given him a real reason to be but that didn't mean he couldn't have his own thoughts on the subject.

Well. Good. That was another sign that she'd gotten deeper into his head than she had thought.

"I got a lot more than ten K, baby," she said.

"Bullshit," he said. "You're full of shit."

"Maybe," she said. "Maybe I am. But that doesn't mean I can't put my hands on that money."

"So? Put hands on it."

"Nothing's changed, Max," she said. "Nicky's still out there. He's probably looking for me right now."

"Yeah, you got problems, all right."

"Not like yours," she said, moving in close.

He might not want to look at her but there were other ways to hold a man's attention.

Her shoulder brushed his and she felt him shift away but that only put his chest against hers. She gave him a thin conspiratorial smile but stayed where she was.

It wasn't seduction, not the kind that makes for sweaty sheets anyway, but it was enough to remind him how small she was, how soft and vulnerable.

"Here's what it is," her words were liquid, warm and inviting as molasses; she could see them seeping in. "Me and Nicky, we got into some shit. There was some drugs and some cash– bags of it– and we got 'em."

"We?"

"I," she said. "I mean I."

He turned to her and looked as if he was about to speak but, instead, brushed past her and headed up the street.

"Damn it," she muttered and followed again.

Above them the clouds were looking heavy and silver, obviously about to drop another deluge on the Harbor. Yet another reason to wrap this up fast.

By the time she caught him he had his cell out and was midway through setting himself up with a bouncer job at some place called Sin City.

Was he kidding? Enough was enough. If she couldn't play his angles, maybe the direct approach was the way to go.

She grabbed his arm, squeezing hard until he was irritated enough to tell his new boss to hold on for a second.

"Yeah?"

"So, that's it, huh?" she said, letting a tiny slice of the shitty mood Nicky had given her bleed through. "You're just gonna walk away? I'm talking about ten thousand fucking dollars, man."

"That's all you do is talk," he said. "You talk but you don't say shit."

"Everybody can't be deep like you, Captain."

"You keep treating me like I got my nose wide open," he said. "I told you about that."

"Look, whatever," she said. "Trust me. Don't trust me. But trust this: I need to get out of the Harbor, tonight. I ain't going without my cash. It's a lot. It's enough to give you what you need to square you with Mrs. Housefire."

He wavered. The possibility that she wasn't

working him, that there really was gold at the end of this rainbow went though his body like a wave and she clocked every ripple.

He wasn't used to trusting anybody and he was pretty much built not to trust her but, at the bottom of things, he was just like any other man- sentimental.

He lived on hope and plans the same way Nicky did, the same way they all did, and, just like every other man in the world, hope was how she would own him.

"You're right," she said, pressing. "I can take my chances and maybe I can do it on my own. Or I can be smart, give you a taste and be sure."

She watched as he almost tipped all the way into the pool she'd filled for him. She could picture the waves of bills, ripples of coins swimming in his eyes.

She knew the lure well; it was the one that had hooked her so many times. Would it hook him, though? He wasn't made like her normal guppies.

"No," he said, shaking his head slightly, seeming to do it more to clear his own mind than to show he wasn't buying. "That's you treating me like a mark again. No."

But it was a weak rebuff, the thinnest yet from him. She knew he was really considering it; she could see him struggling to maintain balance.

It was just too much money and he was in too much need. All he needed was a little shove and tip. She decided to go all in.

"Max," she said in the softest, breathiest version of her voice she held back for these sorts of emergencies. "The question isn't if I'm treating you like a mark. It's why are *you* treating you like one?"

This rocked him again, almost as if he'd been hit. She was nearly home with him. Tip.

"Risky," he was talking to himself. Mulling.

"Risk?" she purred. Soft, innocent, nothing close to sexy, just needing him and hoping. "No, baby. This is a sure fucking thing and you're trying to walk away from it."

She saw him doing the calculation– *how long will it take me to earn that kind of money?*

She saw him counting all the days he'd been out of his son's life– *eight years of desert sand and fear of death and him not knowing the kid even existed.*

It was a lot to make up for, wasn't it? It was a heavy weight.

There you go, Max, she thought. *A little hope goes a fuck of a long way, don't it?*

"Fifteen," he said at last.

"Fifteen?"

"Yeah," he said. "I'll do what you want but for fifteen, not ten."

"Fuck you, fifteen," she said. "I could hire ten guys for that."

"Yeah?" he said. "Then, go get 'em."

It was in that moment that she decided she hated him, just a little bit. Layla had never really believed there were guys like this in the world. Why should she?

She'd met all kinds, after all. Their landscape of thoughts and behavior was as flat and predictable as a sheet of cracked pavement and, by the time she was on her own, just as predictable.

There were two kinds in the world as far as she was concerned: bullies, like Stanis, and marks.

The only trick was in telling who was which. She'd never believed in a third kind.

In fact, after seeing him presented over and over again in the movies and finding not one sliver of an example of the guy in real life, Layla had grown to hate the idea of him. It was that kind of fairy tale that got people, girls especially, fucked.

There was no cavalry. There were no knights. There were no hard guys with hearts of gold out there, just marks and bullies.

Except, now, here was Max.

Fuck you, she thought. *Fuck you for existing.*

"Fine," she said. "Fifteen."

•••

It didn't take them long to get there but, once they had, she insisted they sit outside, watching the joint while she went over things. It wasn't a complex plan but a certain amount of finesse was necessary to carry it off without static.

She was surprised to see how attentive Max became once he'd signed on. He never interrupted, never contradicted, never even offered an alternative to her plan except to ask about the shape and size of the place and what kind of opposition he could expect if things went sour.

It made sense in a way. He was a soldier; he was used to making sure other peoples' plans worked out smooth.

He peered up at the target– a small apartment above what looked like it had once been a butcher shop way back when. It was all boards and tattered yellow DO NOT ENTER signs now, left beyond a billion years ago by some brave city employee.

It seemed to have escaped the Devil's Night scarring shared by so many of the structures on this side of town but Time and Neglect had beat it to hell anyway.

The building, the whole street, smacked of abandonment and decay, even more than the rest of the city.

Gray Harbor was a tough old gal. Most of her was fighting hard against complete collapse but this neighborhood and the others like it that dotted her streets like syphilis scars weren't making the job easier. They had already given up the ghost.

There weren't even any street signs visible to tell where they were; it was like they had driven off the map into a sort of between place, one that didn't quite exist.

Layla shivered a bit and zipped her jacket tight. She didn't want to linger here any longer than she had to either.

"So, you got it, right?" she said, staring up at the window and the feeble glow from what she knew was the result of an anemic floor lamp near the middle of the room. "You don't talk. Let me do that. Just hang by the door and, if things get hinky, shut it down."

"Got it," he said.

"You strapped?" she said.

"Do I need to be?"

"Probably not," she said, mulling. "But you never know."

"Too bad," he said with a shrug. "Should have thought of it before, right?"

"Yeah," she said. "Yeah, right."

"This guy's gonna have to be six kinds of stupid to

just let you walk in there and take your boyfriend's money."

"Seven," she said. "And it's my money. Let's go."

The stairs creaked under them as they climbed up the back way, just as the rear door had when she'd eased it open.

Max took note of the boarded windows, the rusty padlock on the only other exit, the complete lack of cover or maneuvering room in the hallway. He'd been in less helpful places in his life but this one was definitely close to the bottom.

If this shit went crazy while they were bunched up in this dollhouse hallway, he'd have a time getting between her and any trouble. God forbid there was gunplay.

She motioned for him to stop and hang back a bit as they approached the single apartment door. Max noted another window just beyond her at the other end of the short hall.

It was nailed shut, of course, but there was a fire escape barely visible through the grime-encrusted glass.

An ancient fire extinguisher hung precariously in the corner next to the window and had obviously done so since before either of them was born.

Layla tapped his chest, pulling his attention back to her and put her finger to her lips for quiet. Then she knocked.

There was nothing at first, not unless you counted that weird sense of increased quiet when someone you can't see wants you to keep on not seeing them. Max was used to it by now. Somebody was definitely on the other side of the door.

He opened his jacket, showing her the same tire iron she'd used on Reggie before; not much but better than bare knuckles. She nodded and knocked again.

Again there was the odd additional silence lumped onto the rest and then the light behind what Max suddenly realized had been a peephole all this time went dark.

"Layla?" said an unfamiliar voice in a low, raspy whisper.

"Who's it look like?" she said.

"Nicky with you?" said the voice.

"You don't see him here, do you?" she said.

"Who's that with you?" said the voice.

"It's your long lost mother," she said. "Open the fuck up."

The pause before the door opened was just long enough for them to hear seven individual locks being unlatched. Then, when it did open, it was just wide enough for them to get a glimpse of a face– one big dark eye, part of a fire plug of a nose and a mouth that was just on the verge of a growl.

The eye swiveled back and forth, taking them both in, lingering on Max for a few extra moments before narrowing. Max kept his hand tight around the hidden tire iron and was glad for the comfort it gave him.

"Layla?" said the guy with the eye, still glaring at Max.

With an exasperated sigh she shoved the door open, eliciting a grunt from the new guy as it smacked into his face.

She beckoned for Max to follow but when he did, the new guy set himself directly between them, flexing his massive fists in anticipation.

They weren't exactly mirror images– the new guy was bigger, a good decade younger and he was white– but, if you wanted a human brick wall and couldn't find one of these two, the other would do nicely.

Max had chopped down bigger trees but not many and not easily. The new guy already looked like he wanted to take Max's head off.

"Bruno," snapped Layla's voice from somewhere in the apartment. "Quit fucking around."

"I don't know this guy," said Bruno, his eyes never leaving Max. "Nicky said–"

"Nicky ain't here," said Layla. "I'm here."

From where he was, halfway through the front door with the giant slab of angry Bruno in front of him, Max couldn't see where she'd gone.

The place was a bit bigger inside than he'd expected. From the sound it wouldn't surprise him if it took up most of the second floor.

He could hear her rummaging around though, opening what sounded like cabinets and slamming them shut.

"Yeah," said Bruno. "But Nicky said–"

"God damn it," she snapped again. "He's a friend of mine, okay? Jesus. Just get your ass back here and help me."

Obviously disappointed that he wouldn't be able to tear Max's skull off his neck, Bruno moved off. *Nice,* thought Max, stepping in behind him and easing the door shut.

No problems here at all.

While they handled whatever it was they were doing in the back Max did a quick recon of the main room.

Calling it a shithole would have been giving the place more than it deserved.

No one had changed the wallpaper in a good while; it was torn in places and where it wasn't the original colors and pattern had long since faded away.

The light, just a bare bulb at the top of a tall floor lamp, was powered by a small portable generator as was the little fridge and the hot plate. The guy had a few jugs of bottled water set near the window and a sleeping bag rolled nearby.

There was another jug in the bathroom, toothpaste, brush and mouthwash laid out on the sink.

This Bruno was obviously squatting but whether these were his permanent digs or he was just hiding out as part of Layla's big scheme Max neither knew nor cared.

There were no guns around that he could see but Bruno was big enough that he probably never needed one.

The only thing that really caught Max's eye was the big black tarp that had been slung loose over one of the walls. It was new and, as far as Max could tell, wasn't doing much of anything beyond covering the plaster and brick underneath.

He ran a hand over it just to make sure there wasn't a gun rack or a door hidden behind the thing. There wasn't.

It was weird, sure, but not a deal-breaker so Max deemed the place 'safe enough' and set up where he could see Layla and Bruno rooting around in the back.

•••

What in the hell is this? She thought, shifting the

fifth overstuffed bag of what she hoped was just shredded paper.

Bruno had moved past stupid straight to complete idiot with this stunt and she was just on the verge of telling him so.

She'd wanted to get to the bedroom closet and the two duffle bags inside but this moron had taken it in his head to half fill the place with large green garbage bags.

"Layla," said Bruno, sidling closer to her and keeping his voice low. Clearly he had something to say that he didn't want to share with Max.

She swore under her breath as she shifted one set of the stupid bags only to have two more slide down into their place.

"Layla, hey–"

"Bruno," she said, turning on him.

She had some choice things to say to him but she wasn't ready to pull the trigger on his temper yet, not until she had what she wanted in her hands.

After that? Well, if she was lucky, she could wrap this whole thing up.

"Bruno, honey, what the hell is this with all the garbage bags?"

He brightened instantly at that, his wide, blunted features spreading into his version of a smile.

"Smart, huh?" he said. "I thought it up all on my own."

Thrilling, she thought. *Now he's* thinking. *Jesus.*

He slid past her, shifting her gently to one side before wading into the mountain of plastic.

In twos and threes he tossed the bags to the far side of the room until the door to the closet was revealed.

"See," he said. "I figured somebody coming in here would think this was all just trash and they found the wrong place or something. Then they don't even bother with this."

He whipped the closet open only to have another slew of the things slide out like an avalanche.

He tossed them aside too and, when he was done, reached into the dark recesses.

Layla had once loved the old-school design of buildings like this one– the hardwood floors, the hand-crafted moldings, the walk-in closets- now all she wanted was to find the guy she designed this thing, take him up to the roof and toss him off.

"Here," said Bruno, finally hauling the two massive duffles out and dumping them at her feet. "Just like you left them."

She barely heard him. She was already crouched over the nearest bag, tugging the zipper open. Yes. Yes, indeed. This was the heroin, over three hundred little plastic-wrapped bricks of it that added up to a license to print cash.

She reached for the other and, yes, the money, all two hundred and fifty K of it was there as well.

Lovely. Beautiful. Excellent. This was going to work. Everything she'd planned for was actually going to happen. All she had to do now was start tying up the loose ends.

She looked up at Bruno and found him already watching her, that big dumb grin all over his idiot face.

"I like the hair," he said. "The red? It's cool."

"You do, huh?" she said, pulling the zipper closed on the cash. He nodded vigorously. "Well, it's just for you, baby."

"Yeah?"

"Sure," she said. "Everything I do is just for you. Didn't you know that?"

She had him toss the heroin into the other room and flashed Max a smile and a nod when he looked up.

Just hold on, she thought at him. *I'll get to you in a second.*

She stood up and slipped an arm through one of the bag's straps, hauling it onto her shoulder. It was heavy but she only had to manage it down the stairs and into her trunk.

"So," said Bruno, sliding around in front of her. "What now?"

"What now, what?"

"I mean, where are you taking the stuff now? Nicky said—"

"I dunno about Nicky," she said. "But I'm thinking Mexico. Maybe the islands."

She'd lowered her voice to a murmur by then. She wanted this next bit to be just between the two of them. Max would get the news soon enough.

Bruno looked confused which came as no surprise. Layla had always thought of him as sort of a dinosaur with his brain just big enough to keep his body going and not much else.

Ask him anything more complex than his favorite food or color and you might as well have hit him in the head with a two-by-four.

"Whatcha mean, 'islands?'" he said eventually, his voice as low as hers, keeping things close.

He didn't like Max and wasn't swift enough to hide it. She caught Max shifting in the other room and smiled again.

"Well, when the Ivans figure out who boosted their shit, they're gonna come looking," she said. "Me? I don't plan on being anywhere near here when that happens."

Again Bruno's face took on that confused dog quality that made her want to punch him.

"But, I mean, you said Nicky had that covered."

"Did I?"

"Yeah," he said, nodding. "When you told me he was changing the plan and I should bring the stuff here instead of the *Mercy*."

"Wow," she said, grinning at him. "I said a lot, huh? What else did I say, baby?"

"Just, y'know, keep the stuff here until he calls me," said Bruno.

"And why did I tell you that, honey?" she said. It wasn't really nice taxing him this way. She could almost see the steam rising out of his head as the gears inside began to grind against each other.

"You said the Ivans don't know me," he said, squeezing the memory for all he could. "They don't know me so they won't know to look for me and–"

He stopped talking when he saw she was shaking her head.

"I told you to bring the stuff here because I knew anybody trying to take it would have a harder time with you than they would with Nicky."

"But the plan…" The poor thing really was having a time trying to follow her. She almost felt sorry for the big monster. "I mean Nicky said–"

She took his face between her hands and smiled warmly. She could feel the blush rising up in cheeks, fast and hot and watched with amusement as his eyes darted this way and that, desperate to focus on anything but hers.

"Nicky doesn't know where you are," she said, her lips so close to his it was almost already a kiss. "He's out looking all over for you right now. He thinks you fucked him."

That got him.

The last thing on Earth Bruno would ever do was cross Nicky. Not because he was scared of him– Layla doubted Bruno was scared of anyone– but because Nicky had set himself up as some kind of combo of father and big brother in Bruno's world.

It was something that bothered her at first– anyone could tell that Nicky had no more real affection for Bruno than he would for a well-trained fighting dog– but, after a while, when she saw how brutal Bruno was willing to be, how lethal he became if he thought it would put a smile on Nicky's face...

Well. She resolved the best way to handle Bruno was to keep Bruno wanting to handle her. And it worked.

A little touch here, a little flash there, a few greeting card phrases and the big, stupid murderer was hooked on his hunger for her.

She doubted he even had a clear idea what it was she made him feel but, when he started opening up to her about his childhood, about his whackjob of a father, about all that, she knew she had him locked down just as tight as Nicky.

The idea that Nicky thought Bruno might do anything to hurt him hit the big freak like a fist. Good.

"Wait," he said, trying to suss out what he could

have possibly done wrong. "No, I done everything just like you and Nicky said. Why would he–"

She put her hand to his mouth, gently cutting off any more spew. He didn't need to say much now anyway, only listen.

"I know, baby," she said, softly. "I know you'd never fuck Nicky. You want to fuck *me*, don't you?"

Bruno's face went bright scarlet and he looked around as if desperate to find a hole or alcove in which to hide, which was funny because neither of those items came in his size.

Layla stroked his face gently, feeling the heat in him, stoking it.

"Sshhh," she said, still with the murmur, still with the shy little smile. "I know, baby. It's all right. I know how you feel. I've always known."

She could feel Max's eyes on her as she guided Bruno's face close to hers. He had to be wondering what the hell she was playing at. The coldest part of her mind smiled at what she knew would be growing confusion in him as well as Bruno.

For all his bitching about her trying to run some game on him, Max had sure got the idea stuck in his head that Layla was helpless.

Sure, she'd helped him feel that way, nurtured it like one of those exotic plants they used to keep in the city's arboretum, but, on some level, it galled her.

Yeah, she might not be able to bounce guys around on their heads any time she wanted like some people but she was far from fucking helpless.

Watch this, Max, she thought. *Just watch this.*

"It's okay," she said to the monster squirming on her hook. "You love me, right?"

As if hypnotized, Bruno nodded. Her hands continued their easy caress, up and down, up and down his burning cheeks.

"Aw. See? It's okay. And don't you worry about what Nicky's gonna say about it, okay? Know why?"

"Why?" said Bruno as if he was sinking into some beautiful dream.

"Because, baby," she cooed. "The only way a stupid ass, limp dick spud like you would ever get in my pants is if you drugged me, tied me up, blindfolded me and brought in somebody smart to fuck me for you."

Bang.

Bruno jerked away from her as if he'd been struck. Layla watched, a catlike expression of calm on her face, as his brain knotted and un-knotted itself, working out what had just been said.

Nicky had always told her the one thing Bruno could never, ever abide was being called stupid. It was like a trigger that sent him into the sort of berserk rage that usually ended up with somebody in the hospital or the morgue.

Even Bruno's friends weren't spared when he was like that. It was, Nicky said, like giving a chimp a machine gun with the safety off. Bullets would spray everywhere and you just had to hope, when it was empty, that more of your enemies were down than your friends.

And that was when Bruno was idling at zero. After the wind-up she'd just given him she was sure the explosion would be–

Bruno roared like a wounded bear and rushed at her, his hands around her throat faster than she or anybody would have thought possible.

The force of her attack took both of them across the room and slammed her hard into the only wall not covered with those god damned garbage bags. He held her there, by her throat, a foot off the floor, squeezing and babbling about how mean she was and how could she say that when he loved her like he did?

She was just wondering if Max would actually get to her before Bruno put her down for good when he was there.

Bruno only grunted when the tire iron slammed into the side of his head the first time but his grip relaxed enough for her to take one ragged breath. The second hit got his full attention.

With an animal growl he released her, barely noticing as she slid down to the floor, her throat already dotted red from where his fingers had crushed.

Bruno launched himself at Max, hitting him like a boulder from one of those old Warner cartoons. Again, the force of his attack carried them both so fast and hard that Max's back left a little crater in the wall where he hit.

Max was stunned but not enough to keep from bracing his feet against the floor and bringing the iron down again against Bruno's concrete skull. The bigger man staggered a bit and Max pressed in hard, swinging the iron like a bat, connecting every time with the jaw or the chin or the side of his skull.

Bruno took each blow with the same ugly grunt but didn't come close to falling. If anything it seemed the beating gave him focus. He zeroed in on Max after the fifth or sixth hit, completely forgetting about Layla or the money or even his best friend.

203

Max pulled back for another strike, this one aimed at Bruno's neck, but before he could complete the swing, he felt something like a cinder block slam into his chest. It was Bruno's left fist and it knocked the wind out of him.

The iron fell to the floor as Max back-peddled, putting space between him and the monster while he fought to catch his breath.

Bruno wasn't having any, surging forward at Max, swinging wildly so that his blows came like a sort of avalanche.

They didn't always connect, maybe only twice out of five times, but, when they did, Max felt like he was being hit by a car. He needed a little time to get planted and Bruno wasn't giving him any.

His eyes fell on the dropped iron, just sitting there, well within reach if not for the storm of fists between them.

Then he noticed Layla, still lolling against the wall where Bruno had dropped her.

"Layla!" still not quite with them, her head tilted his way and she watched as Bruno pummeled Max into the corner.

There was a window there too, perfect for putting Max's head through if Bruno could get a good grip.

"Layla! Damn it! Get back in the game!"

She shook her head a couple of times and her eyes got bright again. She focused on them, saw the situation and was on her feet scrambling for the iron or the door. Max couldn't tell.

"Oh, no," said Bruno, noticing her as well. "You ain't going no place."

Suddenly Max's face was full of Bruno's palm and

the back of his head was being slammed repeatedly into the wall.

Everything went gray for him for a second and, when he came to, he saw the monster advancing on the girl again, just like in the movies.

Max dived for the iron, snatching it up into a batter's swing as he crossed the tiny distance between them.

Again he went for the homerun against the back of Bruno's skull and, again, all he got was another angry grunt for his trouble.

This time, when Bruno swiveled to face him Max didn't hesitate, didn't set up the next strike. This time he went in like a cane cutter, stroking the iron back and forth across Bruno's face in a quick, vicious cadence.

He smiled when he saw blood on the bigger man's face but wouldn't stop until that face was on the floor.

"Fine," said Bruno, his words slurring as he staggered away from the swinging iron. "That's how you want it. That's how it is."

Bruno fished around behind one the stack of water jugs and suddenly there was a knife in his hand. It was a home-made job from the look of it, a jagged slice of what had once been part of a fan blade now sharpened to a killing edge.

Layla watched them go at it in earnest then, knowing only one of them was going to walk away. It was almost like watching dancers moving through some horrible ballet, swing, miss, duck, kick, swing, spin and on and on each time the blow a little harder or the cut a little closer.

The worst thing was, with them thrashing all over

the place and swinging their toys in every which way, she was rooted where she was.

If she did move she risked catching the wrong end of one of their missed blows or, worse, attracting Bruno's focus.

So she waited and watched and paid no attention whatever to the fact that the door to her little white room was open again and beckoning.

The two men went through a wall together, smashing into the front room and scattering the jugs there.

When they got to their feet Max had lost his iron but Bruno still held the knife tight in his hand.

Layla began to wonder if she had enough time to lug one of the bags to the window and get it down the fire escape before Bruno finished this.

Max was using the jugs for protection now, swinging each like a club until the knife poked through. Then there was water everywhere.

Max had a hell of a time fending off Bruno's vicious swipes and keeping his feet under him at once.

"Where you going now, black man," said Bruno, sliding left or right to block whatever move Max tried to make. "You think you two are gonna work me over? You think I'm dumb? Well, I ain't dumb, you fucking herp. You're the dummy if you think she's gonna stick with you."

"Fuck you, moron," said Max, soberly.

"Don't say that," bellowed the monster, lunging for Max like a storm of murders. "Don't you ever say that!"

The knife went back and forth, up and down, stabbing, jabbing, swiping at Max as Bruno advanced.

Dodging the blade wouldn't have been so hard except for how slippery the water had made everything. It was all over the place now, looking like the aftermath of a broken main.

One slip and Max knew he was done. That slip was inevitable the longer he danced with Bruno. This had to end, quick, or it would end bad for Max. He scanned the room between swipes of Bruno's blade and formed a sort of plan. Desperate, sure, but it was all he had.

There are hundreds of words for stupid and Max went through most of them, working Bruno up into a boiling lather until he was swinging wild on every swipe and paying no mind whatsoever to where their dance took them.

Max had just got around to calling Bruno a half-wit when the monster popped his cork.

Screaming for Max to just *shut up, shut up, shut up,* Bruno launched himself at the smaller man. It was a good move and, had Max not spent the last years grappling with men who thought killing him put them closer to God, he would have had a length of steel embedded in his chest in less time than it took to say.

But Max had been grappling and not one of those men met God on his nickel.

Before Bruno knew what was happening, there was a hand on his wrist and another on his neck guiding him and his blade down. He had just a moment to realize where his knife was headed before he made contact.

He'd bought the little generator on Layla's advice because she didn't know how long he'd have to stay underground. You filled it with a little oil or whatever that stuff was and it kicked out electricity.

It was kind of cool and he had a lot of fun plugging things into it to see how much power it could kick out at once.

As his blade cut through the main cable Bruno felt all that juice surging up through him, sparking his flesh and making all his muscles clench so tight he wanted to scream. It didn't help all that water everywhere and how wet he was.

Electricity, like lightning, arced out of the box, frying him inside and out as the black man and Layla looked on.

He was dead before he knew it.

The last thing he saw was her name peeking out from under the tarp he'd pulled over her special wall.

"Everybody knows this one; They call it the Frog and the Scorpion *or the* Buzzard and the Monkey *or the* Pig and the Crocodile*. It's about how, no matter what's happening in the world around us, at the end of the day we have to be true to our nature. Like we're hard wired to be who we are no matter what. Some people think that's kind of gloomy, like it means you don't have free will or something but, I'm telling you, this meat machine is a happy camper. All I hear in that story is I GOTTA BE ME, y'know. I gotta be me."* – DENNY P, QUICKTREADS ad campaign, autumn 2013

TRACK 14: MAKE ME WANNA DIE

The NO VACANCY light was lit when they got back to the motel meaning all of Halo's ponies were running. It also meant the greasy bastard was likely nodding off in his office with dreams of cash and condoms in his head.

They opted for Layla's room, figuring it was the last place Nicky would look for her but Max was so keyed up he checked the closets and the bathroom before he would let her inside.

"Jeez," she said, hauling the second duffle in. "You ain't half cautious, are you?"

"Are you crazy?" he said, exploding. He'd been brick quiet for the entire drive back but now he was erupting. "Are you out of your God damned mind?"

"Take it easy, Max," she said flopping down on the bed.

"My ass," he said, now pacing back and forth like a caged bear. "That fucker tried to kill us."

"Max, really," she said, kicking off one of her sneakers. "Take it easy. It's done."

"Fuck that," he said. "Fuck that. That fucker- what was his name?"

"Bruno."

"Bruno," he said like he was eating the name. "He didn't know what was going on, did he? God damn moron had no clue."

"Max..." "I thought you said you was partners with him," said Max.

"Nicky," said Layla, kicking off the other shoe. It was nice to feel her toes again. "Nicky was partners with him. I told you."

"No," he said, whirling on her. "No. You said it was you. We're just supposed to walk in, pay the fucker off and split. What the hell did you say to him to set him off like that?"

"Nothing, Max," she said. "Nothing."

He grabbed her, hauling her to her feet so they were face to face. She'd never seen him like this and she'd never had his eyes on her like that. She didn't like it.

"What did I tell you about treating me like a mark?" he said and there was a real threat under the words.

"You're hurting me."

Max looked down at where his hand gripped her arm. He could feel her bicep shifting like soft rubber under his fingers. He let her go and backed off. She watched as his eyes went flat again and he returned to his normal granite state.

"Look, I'm sorry," she said, rubbing her arm. She let him keep his distance. "I had no clue he'd go off like that. I told you he was kind of twitchy."

"'Twitchy?'" said Max. "You call that homicidal, Creature Feature shit 'twitchy'?"

She smiled. "That's why I wanted you there. It was me he went after first, remember?"

That was true. Max had only stepped in when the monster went homicidal on her and that was the reason she'd hired him, right? To keep folks like him off her back.

"Yeah," he said after he'd chewed it a bit. "Yeah.

Okay."

"So, we're cool?" she said, dropping down next to the first duffle. He nodded. "Good, because you need to be in a good mood when you see this."

Without waiting for a response, she unzipped the bag, revealing the bricks of H inside. Max had seen lots of drugs in his life but mostly in the hands of users, just a joint here or a vial there. This was enough to keep the C Section floating for a good week. Maybe more.

"What you planning on doing with all that?" he said and it was clear that any answer other than 'tossing it in the bay as soon as possible' would not satisfy.

"I dunno," she said, zipping it up quick and moving to the other. "Salvation Army?"

"You can't sell that shit, Layla," he said. "Money's one thing. But that–"

"Hey, ease up Captain," she said, "You only been on the dark side for an hour. You don't get to lecture me on what to do with my stuff."

That pulled him up short. *The dark side?* Was that where he was now? He'd spent his whole life, well, most of it, trying to walk the straight middle line. It wasn't easy, especially when the Law said one thing and Doing Right went against it but he'd managed, in his mind, to stay true. Now she was saying he'd crossed over?

If he had, he didn't feel any different. He went into the bathroom and checked his face but, aside from the bruise Bruno had pounded into his temple, it was the same one he expected to see. Same old Max.

So, had he crossed over, like she said, or was his

213

face telling him the goods? If she was wrong, if he hadn't stepped too far into the dark, then where was he now? He thought of Bruno, his skin burnt mottled and black, lying on the floor of that dead apartment. Who would find him? No one. Who would mourn him? Max had no clue. Was it a murder or had Max been simply protecting himself? Was this even his fault? Who had set the events in motion? Who had brought him there in the first place? Who had put herself in a position to have not one but two men out for her blood?

"Dude," said Layla's voice from the other room. "You totally have to see this."

Her jacket was off when he returned to her as well as her socks and she'd tossed the red hooker wig aside revealing the close cut blond beneath. It was funny but, without all the extra crap, she was kind of cute. Still on the skinny side, but cute.

The second bag open now with about a third of its contents spread all over the bed. Even that third– all in hundreds, he noticed– was more than he had seen in one place at one time. And where had all that come from? A million drug deals in a million back alleys and city parks? Was the money green now or gray like the city around them? What color was Max, after all this?

He shook his head to clear it of all the doubts. Terrance was all that really mattered now. He wanted to see his son, to be his father if the kid would have him. There was only one road to that and it went straight through Reggie.

Layla wiggled her toes at him playfully.

"I'll take my cut now," he said.

"Are you nuts," she said, rolling her body around in the money, tossing handfuls of bills at him like wedding bouquets.

"Think I'm gonna get moving," he said. "So, I'll need my cut."

"See, that's your trouble, Captain," she said, watching him upside down from beneath her pile of Franklins. "You don't know how to celebrate."

"Celebrate?" he said. "With you?"

"Why not me," she said and then, seeing his expression, quickly added. "Look, Max. I know you got things to do but I'm on my ass until that last bus out of here."

"Not taking the car?"

"Would you?"

No, he thought. *Not with all that cash and a psycho boyfriend stalking me. Better to get a rental a few stops up the line.*

"So that's like three hours from now," she said, flipping over into a kneel. "You can stick with me for another three hours, can't you? Besides, the deal was you shadow me 'til I get out of town, right?"

"Right," he said.

"Well, then," she said, shoving some bills into his hand and holding them and it in hers. She was warm. So was he all of a sudden. "When I catch my bus, you get your cut."

"And what do we do for three hours?" he said. A second later her shirt was off and he was looking at her little blue star. "Oh, it's like that, is it?"

"Yeah," she said, reaching for him. "It's just like that."

He was inside her fast, hard, all hammers and pistons, lava rippling under his skin. She gasped at the suddenness of it, the almost familiar way her body opened to him, rolled against him like that warm Waimea surf in her memory.

His mouth on hers, hot, almost desperate, drinking her like desert water, her lips on his, her tongue in him, her fingers clawing his back, to hurt him or hold him or both.

It scared her at first; he did, his way with her. It wasn't the fear Nicky put in her at the end of his belt or that hot, stinging, barbed wire terror that Carlos unrolled on her when the tequila got thin.

She didn't have a name for it, the frosty, burning thing he made of her as she ground her belly against him, panting into his mouth.

Shit, maybe there wasn't a name for it; maybe no one but she had ever felt this thing, this twisty, wrenching hot-cold thing or, if they had, maybe they knew it couldn't be named. Some things couldn't.

She groaned as the first tremors rippled through her, her thighs clamping his flanks, her heels driving him into like a storm. He groaned back, into her, a long low growling thing that was half hunger and half release.

Maybe it wasn't even fear. Maybe she'd got so used to squashing down all the terrors, all the frights, little and big but, whatever it was, it was all over her now, all in her, was her.

She was gone after that, out somewhere past her safe white room, somewhere where her thoughts turned to steam and all there was left of her was muscles and teeth and wet inside and out.

Whatever he was, wherever he was inside, if he had a white room of his own where he kept safe, or a space beyond where he could disappear too, she didn't know and didn't care.

She *wasn't* anymore which was fine by her. No more Layla, for even a moment, was so much more than fine it was almost like love.

There was comfort in being gone that way and she took it, over and over, until she was a wisp of herself, a soft perfect cloud on a winter sky, white on white on white on white.

"Damn," he said after a few minutes. She lay panting next to him, covered in both their sweat, her chest heaving with his as she pulled her breath back into its normal cycle.

"Wow," she said.

"Been a long time, huh?" he said.

"Long time since it was like that," she said. He could tell she meant it and he felt the same way. Weird. "That was fucking great."

"Yeah."

"Too bad we're never seeing each other again after tonight," she said.

"Yeah," he said. "Too bad."

With a kittenish little sigh she rolled over onto him, her blue star pressed flat against his chest.

"You mind?" she said softly.

He didn't. It was coming up twilight outside and the room was dark enough to need the glow from one of the lamps.

He didn't reach for it just yet, preferring to watch her as she moved milk- white in the thickening shadow.

217

She lay her head down against him, pressing an ear to his chest.

"I can hear your heartbeat," she said.

"Yeah?" She nodded, her hair brushing back and forth, tickling him into a smile. "What's it sound like?"

She made the familiar *lub-dub* sound followed by a pretty good impression of a car engine revving. He laughed. She laughed and he thought it was probably the first true thing to come out of her mouth since he'd met her.

"Can I ask you something?" she said after a little.

"Like what?"

"Like what made you bust in on Nicky and me last night?"

Jesus. Was that only last night? He'd been shot and bounced around so much since then if felt like a lifetime ago. Another lifetime.

"Heard the whole thing through the wall," he said. "Him working you over."

She blushed at that, remembering and pulled herself closer to him.

"Yeah," she said. "But you didn't have to do nothing about it."

"It wasn't right," he said and there was a finality to it as if he'd added 'the end' right after.

"A lot of people see a lot of shit that ain't right," she said, "And they don't do jack."

"That's true."

"But not you," she said.

"Guess not."

She was up on her elbows then, staring into his eyes. Scanning him, he thought.

"So what makes you so special, Captain?"

"I ain't nothing special," he said.

"Nicky could have turned around and shot you."

"Shit," he said. "That punk ain't got the juice to shoot nobody. Not while they looking at him."

"Maybe," she said. Her eyes were really digging into him now, like little lasers. "But you didn't know that. What if he had a gun or something?"

"He didn't."

"Yeah," she said, frowning a bit. "But what if he did?"

In response, he shifted a bit, reaching over to where his jacket had been tossed on the floor. He fished around inside for a moment before coming back with that familiar bit of taped paper.

"Ah, shit, Max," she said. "I already read that shit before. Just talk to me."

So he talked; he read from the paper and, though it irritated her to hear it, listening to him speak the words was different than just reading them had been.

Before they had been just dead blots of ink filling some white space, useless in her mind unless they could get her something concrete.

But now, as he spoke, the words took a different shape, a solid one with hooks that reached into her and, despite the smooth icy caste on her heart, managed to find a little purchase.

"We are not enemies, but friends," he said, the soft rubble of his voice vibrating through his chest and into her. "We must not be enemies. Though passion may have strained, it must not break our bonds of affection. The mystic chords of memory, stretching from every battlefield and patriot grave to every living heart and

219

GEOFFREY THORNE

hearthstone all over this broad land, will yet swell the
chorus of the Union when again touched, as surely
they will be, by the better angels of our nature."

When he was done she lay there against him,
feeling his heart, watching the shadows make the
room blacker.

"You don't get it," he said at last. "Do you?"

"Nope," she said. "Guess not."

"It's simple," he said. "The Better Angels, that's
us."

She laughed, not unkindly but with real
amusement. Was he kidding? What kind of angel
could she ever be? He was joking or he was out of his
fucking mind.

"Try to be good, right?" he went on, taking no note
of her laugh. "That's it. All this shit, the world, I
mean, it's us. Good folks and bad folks and in-
between. You ain't gotta be perfect. You ain't gotta be
no saint. You just gotta try. Try to be good. That's it."

That's it, huh? she thought.

For him it obviously was. She could see him in her
mind all of a sudden, like one of those soldiers on the
news. He was standing in the desert somewhere, wind
blowing, sand all over everything, one of those weird
flat army trucks tooling around nearby.

Somebody gives him a note or he gets an
unexpected call and it's the big news: *you got a son,
Max. You got a little boy you didn't know about for
eight fucking years.*

She could see him getting worried, his big stone
face going soft, his deadly implacable reflexes dulled
for the first time maybe ever.

She saw him in fear for his life for the first time

ever because now he had something to get back to. She saw those last few weeks or months like sliding through hell for him. And she saw him get through it all on nothing but grit.

Must be nice, she thought. *I mean, look at him. He's big. He can handle himself. I bet he could eat fucking nails. But everybody ain't like that. Some people have to live in the shit. Some people gotta eat it. Some people gotta get knocked on their ass and come up smiling so they don't get knocked down again.*

Suddenly she was thinking of what she would do if she was Max. She thought of how'd she be in her life if she had been him this whole time. Maybe she'd have burned down a crack house or two. Sure. Maybe she'd have even saved Jumper and married him and moved into the Barbie Dream House for the rest of her life.

"I wish it was that easy," she said at last. Her voice sounded strange to her, hollow, as if coming from a great distance.

"I said, 'simple,'" said Max gently. "Didn't say nothing about 'easy.'"

Fucker, she thought and she punched him in the side.

"Hey," he said, jolting upright and knocking her out of position. "What was that for?"

"Lie down, Max," she said and the way she said it made him do it.

She lay against him again in the dark, thinking new thoughts. After a little he asked her what they should do with the last hour and ten before her bus appointment?

She climbed on top and gave him an idea.

The shower felt good after all that action. The hot water opened his muscles up again, smoothing away the aches and bruises.

He didn't feel gray anymore either which surprised him.

He felt like his old self– his old, Old Self– the one before the fire, before his escape and definitely before his return. He felt young again. He felt clean.

As he dried himself and rolled on the deodorant he pictured the look on Reggie's face when he showed up with the cash.

There were so many ways he could do it, too, each one making her think twice before spouting off the next time.

It was strange feeling hopeful again but he thought he could get used to it.

"Hey," he yelled out to her as he pulled on his shirt. "Too bad you got to roll out. You're gonna miss seeing Reggie when I hand off all this loot. One day later? She is going to trip the hell out."

There was no response from the other room but he was too occupied with his belt buckle and shoes to notice. He did prick up at the sound of the door opening and closing. Was she running out on him? He couldn't believe it; not after last night. Still, it wouldn't hurt to be sure.

"Hey," he said, stepping into the main room. She was just sitting there in the bed, wrapped in the sheets and looking a lot like she'd seen a ghost. "What's up? You having second thoughts or something?"

Something moved behind him, a shadow in his

periphery, and he turned towards it.

"Or something," said Nicky.

It was Nicky, skinny, punk ass Nicky, standing there like he owned the place.

Then it was the tire iron, hard across Max's skull.

Then it was black.

Everything was black.

Everything was.

Everything.

"It is said that if you know your enemies and know yourself, you will not be imperiled in a hundred battles; if you do not know your enemies but do know yourself, you will win one and lose one; if you do not know your enemies nor yourself, you will be imperiled in every single battle." – **Sun Tzu, The Art of War**

TRACK 15: TWISTIN' THE NIGHT AWAY

He woke up in the dark and remembered.

He remembered the feel of the tire iron smashing into his jaw. He remembered the stench of drugstore aftershave mixing with the aroma of disinfectant.

He remembered the voices as hands took hold of him and dragged him from somewhere to somewhere else.

...the fuck you looking at? That was Nicky. *Get your goddamn clothes on. I can't move this gorilla by myself, can I?*

He remembered how his head screamed as the blood rushed in and he was tossed into somebody's trunk.

...yeah, monkey boy, Nicky again. *See how you like it, you herp motherfucker .*

He remembered the hood coming down. There was music drifting in from somewhere- the car's radio, he guessed.

Somebody was listening to *Journey*. Then there were more voices, well, maybe the same one, floating in from the same unseen somewhere. ...

When Stanis shows up you don't say shit, right? Nicky again. Always Nicky. *Not a fucking peep. Same with that psycho, Gregor. He says boo to you it's cause he wants to get in your pants so just hang back and let me handle it, yeah? Just act like a stupid fucking piece of ass and you'll do all right. That won't be hard for you anyway. Method acting, right? Right?*

Maybe there was another voice out there making
yes or okay noises but his brain was too liquid to sort
it all out. Nicky's voice was the only solid anchor and
he clung to it, hoping it would be enough to haul him
back to himself again.

*...So, fucking Bruno's still un- fucking-findable.
Spent all day looking for him. Nothing. Don't know
what the hell would make him cut out like that. Moron.
You got any ideas on that...*

Something hit the car or it rolled over something or
whatever. In any case the jolt sent him tumbling back
down into the black and had to fight again to crawl
back up.

*...You fucked that monkey, didn't you? Yeah, you
did. Fucking bitch...*

It was no use. Black was all and it was him and he
was tumbling, tumbling, tumbling down.

•••

The water hit his face like a giant's slap and he was
suddenly out of the black and back in his skin.

The first thing he knew was that half his face was
screaming at him to get some God damned painkillers,
fast, and not that over-the-counter crap, either–
weapons grade stuff.

The second thing he noticed or, rather, the second
thing his brain could process as it came out of the fog,
was the giant warehouse that seemed to have grown
up around him.

There were crates and steel shipping containers all
over and the ugly stink of filthy water in his nose so
he knew he was near the docks.

"Welcome back," said Nicky, making himself the

third and most important thing in his mind.

Layla was nowhere to be seen; he still wasn't enough himself to know if he thought that was good or bad.

"Bet you never saw this coming, did you, Monkey Boy?"

Max had to admit he didn't. Waking up in Gray Harbor, right on the actual body that gave the place its name, shackled to a chair while some lunatic danced around him brandishing a tire iron was, maybe, dead last on his list of expectations.

He was almost happy when the blackness reached up to grab him. Then there was another slap of cold water against him and he wasn't so happy again.

"Nope, we gotta talk," said Nicky. "I need to tell you how this is gonna go."

Max was pretty sure he had a good idea how this was going to go and wondered why he couldn't just be slowed to slide back down again. It wasn't like he'd be around much longer anyway, right?

"So, here it is," said Nicky, warming to the subject. "I'm gonna have to mess you up pretty bad. See, you're s'posed to be Bruno and you just ain't. So, I can't have you talking to Stanis about that.

The bad news is that things're gonna go pretty much down hill after that. Stanis is gonna want to talk to you about his money and his drugs and, since you won't be able to talk, well, it's not gonna be fun. Sorry."

He heard something scuttling off to the side where the shadows were thickest. What was it about landlords that kept them from putting good lighting into joints like this? The rats certainly weren't scared

229

of the dark.

He tossed his head to that side and was rewarded with a glimpse of Layla, pretty blond Layla in her tee and her jeans, hugging the shadow like an old friend. He could see the guilt on her face, sparkling like a glitter tattoo.

He was just thinking how much she deserved to feel that way, how much worse she could stand to feel when the dark reached up for him again.

"Hey," said Nicky, slapping him. Apparently there was no more water. "Stick with me here, chief. You're in enough trouble as it is."

Max struggled to stay up but wasn't sure why? The black was the best place for him now, the safest and, most of all, freest of pain. But he did stay up, for Nicky and for Layla too. Let her see what she bought him. She should see that.

"You fucked her, didn't you?" Nicky was right his face, hissing his words like some kind of python. "I won't lie to you, man. Just the idea that a fucking jungle animal like you could even put his hands on my girl makes me want to puke all over you but, the thing is, I had to get you here to take Bruno's place."

Max laughed. It was an ugly thing, full of broken teeth, but the idea of him taking Bruno's place just tickled him considering how totally dead Bruno was at the moment and how likewise Max would be soon. Funny. You had to laugh.

Nicky didn't see the humor, of course. Max could tell a laugh was not the way to win him over just now but he couldn't help himself.

"Yeah, right," said Nicky. "Keep that up."

Then he broke off, stalking over to where she

230

stood, watching, and dragged her back, close. His hands were under her shirt, down the back of her pants, all over, and she just stood there talking it, looking at Max with that strange mix of guilt and...

...he didn't know what the other thing was.

The black was calling him again. It was just a whisper but he knew it would grow.

"How's this for funny, Monkey Boy?" said Nicky, holding her close. "You know everything she said was a lie, right? You know everything she ever says is a lie. She's mine, man. All mine. And even though she's gonna pay for letting you at the cookies, trust me, I know she did it all for me."

Nicky asked Max if he had anything to say at that point, something in the vein of Last Words because, frankly, that's what they were going to be.

Max had nothing to say.

"Okay," said Nicky with a genial shrug. "Have it your way."

Then he pulled a very nice set of brass knuckles out of his pocket. He still had the one good hand after all.

•••

"Welcome back," said Nicky, taking the bottled water Layla offered. "Don't worry. I'm not walking out on you. Just taking a little break before the Ivans get here."

He chugged the water down and tossed the bottle. Layla stood nearby still with the half miserable, half whatever-it-was look on her face. Max took the same pleasure that what she'd done was

backing up on her a little but he wished he could decipher that other bit. What the hell was that?

Nicky looked up at him from where he was

toweling off and caught the focus of Max's gaze. He smiled and joined her there where Max could see.

"Man," he said, still acting the good old friend. "You got some fucked up luck, don't you?

He smacked Layla one when she tried to pull off, embarrassed maybe that Max would see how far down she was, how much Nicky really owned her, then pulled her close, laughing.

"I mean, first you get born a monkey," he said, between kisses. "That ain't your fault, I guess. But then you get all twisted up over some crackhead jungle bitch."

His hands were all over her again, under her clothes, over, everywhere. His lips were on hers, on her cheek, on her throat. He was obviously putting on a show for Max, taunting him.

"Yeah," he said, keeping one eye on Max the whole time. "She told me the whole story. I gotta say, man. My heart goes out to you. When you get fucked, you really get fucked."

She wasn't pulling away so much now and Max was getting sick. The tiny bit of guilt he thought she felt was gone now and she was just this thing in his hands that he was working, like a puppeteer, for Max's benefit.

"I figure," said Nicky, slowly inching her shirt up towards her breasts even as she half-heartedly struggled to keep it down. "The least we can do is give you one last show. I mean, you're never gonna get a taste of anything like this after Stanis is done with you."

After that Nicky's mouth was too full of Layla to keep up with the taunts but he still kept the one eye on

Max making sure their captive audience caught every bit of his show.

And Max did watch, every touch, every moan and bend because, even if he was a complete little shitheel, Nicky was right. This was about as close as he was going to get again.

The two lovers began to really go at it. Now Layla wasn't bothering to fight Nicky; her hands were all over him too, down his jeans, under his shirt, playing him like a trumpet just as he played her.

"You watching, monkey?" said Nicky, his voice thick with lust. "Bet you get a boner watching this. Fucking animal."

She shushed him with a deep kiss, drawing his attention back where it belonged: on her. Max hated himself for not being able to turn away, to stop himself form listening but it was like he was transfixed.

The whole thing was so surreal it flowed over his mind like a dream. Maybe it really was just a dream. Maybe he was still asleep, back at the *Mercy* with Layla pushed up under him and the bags of cash at their feet.

"Told him," said Nicky, cutting into Max's fantasy like a buzzsaw.

"Mm?" she said, soft into his neck between kisses. "Told him what, baby?"

"Teach him to put his monkey hands on my shit," he grabbed her ass hard, digging his fingers in. "That's you, dumbass."

"Nicky," she moaned, writhing on his hands, against his crotch. "Baby?"

"Yeah," he said, letting her do as she liked. Her

hands were everywhere– running through his hair, under his shirt, in his jacket. "Yeah, what?"

"Remember what I said?"

"Um," he moaned as one of her hands went into his briefs, scratching the flesh there the way he liked. "Remember what?"

He groaned and, for the first time, took his eye off Max.

"What I told you...," she whispered, the vibration in her lips thrumming against his skin.

"Told me?" he said, clearly not giving a shit what she was talking about as long as she kept it up. "About what?"

"About the next time you put your hands on me," she said, nuzzling him and grinding against his body. Her hands were everywhere again and he was getting lost.

"Oh, yeah," he said, smiling. He even chuckled a bit. "Said you was gonna kill me, right?"

"Right," she said and then the knife, the one Stanis had left him, the one he'd kept close in his jacket's inner pocket, was out, open and in her hand.

Before either Nicky or Max could process what was happening, the gleaming silver blade was plunging in and out of Nicky's throat.

There was a spray of blood, nothing like the fountain they show in the slasher flicks but enough for everyone present to know Nicky was done.

Layla skipped backwards to keep it off her as Nicky clawed at the knife that had killed him.

It was no use. He managed to croak out one last, "You bitch," before pitching forward on his face– done.

Again Max wasn't sure he wasn't dreaming. The blood was everywhere, spattering him and the floor and her like a Rorschach.

He watched her as she leaned back against one of the warehouse's big support struts, shock and disbelief fighting for control of her features.

They both lost out to some other emotion, something cold and hard that Max was glad he couldn't name.

He watched as she moved back towards Nicky's body, stood over it for a second– maybe to convince herself he really was dead– and then she started kicking.

"Motherfucker," she said with every impact of her foot against him. "Motherfucker, motherfucker, motherfucker, motherfucker."

Then, when she'd kicked herself out and, maybe, when she really was sure he really was dead, she began to cry.

Max watched her, mute, as great shuddering sobs wracked her body over and over, building to some kind of crescendo and then, for no reason that he could see, just stopped.

She bent down next to Nicky's body then, kissed him lightly on the cheek and said, so softly that Max almost missed it, "Now look what you made me do."

Then she stood up straight, pulled her jacket back on and zipped up tight. She was just about to drag Nicky's body off somewhere when she noticed Max, still watching her.

He couldn't speak yet, Nicky had done too good a number on him, just as promised but his eyes pleaded with her.

All she had to do was get the knife and cut the ropes that held him. All she had to do was let him go. She owed him that much, right.

"Nope," she said after a second or two. "Sorry. Forget it."

She dropped the body where it lay and walked out of sight. Max listened to her dwindling footfalls until he was sure she was gone.

He was alone with the corpse and the blood and– the knife! She hadn't taken it. It was still right where she'd left it, halfway into Nicky's throat.

Summoning up everything he had left Max strained against his chair, inching it in hard little hops toward the corpse. Every part of him screamed for him to stop– the ropes gouging into his wrists and ankles, whatever Nicky had left him of his jaw, the shame he felt for falling for Layla's grift– but he pressed on. There was no way, no way he was going out like this.

He made it about halfway to Nicky's body before the chair fell over.

He was done. He had no strength left for another try even if the chair had been back on all four legs. Done.

The Ivans would be there soon and, the sick joke of it was, everything Nicky had predicted for him would still come to pass.

They might puzzle at the dead body keeping him company but they'd still want to get answers out of Max and they'd be just as sweet about asking if not worse.

He lay there, trying to steel himself for it, trying to call up the black at least so he'd be gone into it before the Ivans got to work but it was useless. All he could conjure up was the name of a little boy he'd never met, whose face he would never see.

He had no idea how long he lay there, smelling the stink of blood and sewage but it wasn't long enough.

He heard footfalls approaching and knew that the rest of his life could be measured in minutes.

There wasn't enough left of him to fight them and there damned sure wasn't enough left to survive their questions.

The footfalls drew closer, louder.

Good-bye, Terrance. Good-bye, son. I'm so sorry I never–

"Jesus," said Layla. "What the hell am I doing?"

He couldn't see her, his position on the floor had him facing into nothing but a massive shadow, but he heard her cross to where Nicky was and he felt it when she came up behind him and began cutting the ropes.

He wanted to speak, to thank her, to tell her he hadn't given up but it just came out as a series of ugly burbling croaks.

"Shut up," she said. "Just shut up. I was home free, you sonofabitch. The Ivans don't know me. I got all the loot and all the drugs. I got my car and I got–" She stopped for a moment as his hands came free and then moved down to his legs. "Nobody knows me, Max. Nobody knows I'm alive, except you. Except you."

Then his legs where free and he was moaning from the pain as circulation returned.

She helped him up, grumbling the whole time about her amazing scam and all the shit she'd eaten to pull it off.

Nicky hadn't come up with any of it; it had all been Layla, making little suggestions, pumping up his ego, staying out of sight, even taking the beatings he dished out, all because she knew the could outlast the stupid wannabe wiseguy and skate with the loot.

"You think I'm just some little tweaker slut, likes to get her block knocked off?" she said as she used a torn bit of her shirt to wipe some of the blood off him. She handed him one of the remaining water bottles and watched him drink. "That's what he thought too, the stupid shit. That's what I fed him for a fucking year. The whole thing almost goes to hell when Gregor showed up early but, damn it, I still pulled it out. And then what happens?"

"What?" he said, regretting it right away. The water helped his throat but his jaw still hurt like hell. Broken probably.

"You happened, Max," she said. "You."

He was apologizing for whatever it was he'd done and she was telling him to shut up when they both heard the sound of a car pulling up outside.

"Shit," she said. "The fucking Ivans."

"Look. I'm just one guy. I got my own family to look out for too, my own life. So I know, even if I prove to you that all of us will come out ahead on this, you're going to have to look out for your own interests as you see them. They may not line up. To you they might not. I get it. All I can say is people do better, we do better, when we can look at the big picture and work for the same thing. People talk about human nature. They make it like all we do is tear each other down, first chance we get. But look around you. This is a city. A real, living city, still. People built it. People make it go. People, together. The less we do that, the more it dies. And it's dying. We all agree on that. So look around, okay. Take a walk in the streets; talk to a bartender or a cop. See it. Think about what going for yourself is gonna get you and then see what we can do if we just put the crap aside and cooperate." – **Councilman Gerard Woodman, public address to the Gray Harbor City Council, Dec. 18, 2011**

TRACK SIXTEEN: VIRGIN STATE OF MIND

Gregor wasn't happy but Stanis was used to that. Gregor was rarely happy unless he had his hands in something wet. Gregor had never liked Nicky and had been against Stanis' little test to see if he could measure up.

He had wanted to kill Nicky fast– well, faster than normal– just to be done with the little bastard but that wouldn't have got Stanis his money back.

If there was one thing he's learned before leaving the cold embrace of Mother Russia it was to keep his eyes focused hard on the money. Outside of family, nothing else mattered, nothing.

But Gregor had been right about Nicky so far so, as soon as he delivered Bruno and as soon as Bruno delivered Stanis's H and cash back to him, Gregor would get his wish. He would get his wish with Bruno too but that was just business; this thing between him and Nicky was personal somehow in a way that Stanis couldn't really understand.

Ah well.

He had half expected Nicky to try and run. About half of them did, thinking something as insignificant as a few hundred miles could keep Stanis off them. Silly. American.

He was gratified to see the one car parked in the otherwise empty lot of the otherwise empty warehouse he kept for this sort of thing.

Wet stuff. He kept it for the wet stuff.

He was less gratified to find the scene of carnage waiting for them when they made their way inside.

"Ah, shit," said Gregor, after giving the corpse the once-over. "Somebody did the little fucker first."

"This Bruno, you think?" said Stanis. Gregor nodded, his mind on other things.

For his part, Stanis was concerned with the set pieces, the furniture, the bloody floor, the knife he'd given Nicky for safekeeping. Something was not right here. The whole thing looked a bit, what was the word– *artificial*– to his eyes.

Yes, Nicky was dead but who had killed him and why with the knife? Why drag the body in a rough circle around the place, smearing blood everywhere but not take it away? Why not hide it or clean the mess? This was amateur work, for sure, and that meant there was more here to discover.

Amateurs were sloppy; they made too many mistakes to live long so it followed that everything they needed to track this one or these ones down was still right here with Nicky.

There was no sign of another car. There was no sign of another weapon. The knife had been dropped on the floor near to the overturned chair where someone had cut some ropes. The floor was covered in blood but only in that odd circle that led from Nicky's body back to Nicky's body.

"So much blood," he muttered, thinking. "So much blood but no footprints. Not one."

Someone had cleaned here. Someone had cleaned here but they had been hasty. They had been hasty to hide their own footprints but not to conceal Nicky.

Why?

There were many places to stash a body here. Or maybe there were not.

The few shipping containers they kept here to make the place look active were empty all right but sealed shut. The padlocks were still intact. The crates were open enough and there were many but ten minutes of looking proved all of them empty as well. That left only the lockers.

Nicky was small but not small enough to fit inside one of those thin metal things So why was there a smudge of blood beneath them? Why was there the one single tiny smudge near the lockers when someone had been so careful as to clean up everywhere else?

Stanis drifted past Gregor who was occupied tossing Nicky's body into one of the wooden crates and setting the lid on top.

"Gregor, my old friend," said Stanis. "I do believe we have a guest here."

"You're kidding," said Gregor, not at all sure what the boss was on about now. The scowl on his face told Stanis he was still fuming over being denied his chance to get Nicky alone.

"Yes," said Stanis. He then leaned in towards the lockers, almost bowing to them, and began to speak. "Hello, my friend. Won't you come out of your box and join us? Are you shy? Are you afraid of what we will do? Come out and we will talk. I tell you, it will be better for you if you come out. It can be quick at least."

Nothing moved, of course. Sometimes Gregor thought Stanis was a little balmy.

"Gregor," said Stanis. "This door, please."

Yes. Crazy as a gulag rat but still the boss. Gregor left off stuffing Nicky into the crate and joined Stanis by the lockers. They weren't actually locked as it turned out so the door wasn't really an issue. Stanis just didn't like to get his hands dirty.

"Hey," said Gregor when he'd pulled the door open. "It's a girl."

"Yes," said Stanis, reaching out a gentlemanly hand to the little blond thing. She looked terrified, poor dear. "A girl is just what it is."

"Who are you?" they asked her. Nobody. She was nobody. They assured her that she was somebody, certainly she was to

them, and it would be much better if she gave them her name. "Layla," she said eventually.

Stanis told her he thought she looked like a little mouse. He smiled and suddenly he seemed like a kindly old man instead of a doorway into an abattoir.

"I am Stanis, Layla," he said, playing the genial father. "This is Gregor. Do you know us?"

She said she didn't. She said she didn't know anything about anything. Stanis told her he was certain she did know something; she knew enough to hide in the locker after all.

"There is all this blood here, Layla," he said. "And this dead man." Gregor snorted at that but stopped when Stanis shook his head. "So, tell me, please, what has happened to you here?"

Layla began to speak but Stanis put up a hand.

"No," he said. "The truth."

She began again and, again, the hand came up.

"No," he said again. "Tell me the truth. That is all I

want, Layla. It is the easiest thing."

So, she told them.

She told them about her boyfriend, Nicky. She told about his friend Bruno and how they got into an argument about some bags or some money or something. She told them about how Nicky called Bruno an idiot and how that set Bruno off like a rocket.

She told how Bruno went berserk, killing Nicky with the knife and how he dragged the bags out to his car. She told how she thought Stanis and Gregor were Bruno coming back in to kill her too and how she had scrambled to hide herself. Then she cried, she cried a lot, and Stanis handed her his handkerchief.

"Stay here, Layla," said Stanis and drew Gregor off to have a private chat. "You don't move, yes?"

She nodded, dabbing her eyes dry and obviously doing her best not to show how shit scared she was, how out of her depth. Stanis gave her a warm smile as she stepped into the shadows with Gregor. She wasn't stupid enough not to try to smile back.

"This story," he said when they were out of her earshot. "How does it sound to you?"

"I dunno," said Gregor. "It's possible, maybe. I guess."

"She is pretty, no?" said, Stanis, glancing back at the stricken girl. "She reminds me of my youngest. Illyana. Around the eyes."

Stanis had made up his mind so Gregor waited as he went back to the girl.

"May I say something to you?" he said, crouching down beside her. "You are a nice girl. A good girl, I think."

245

"Thanks," she said and sniffled.

"You see this blood," he said.

She made a show of looking, yes, of course she could see it. Her eyes were as big as headlights in her face, wide and shining like glass.

He smiled again, the Santa Claus one, and gently took her hand.

"This, this life, it's not for you," he said. "Go out of here. Forget this moment. Throw it away. Find a man. Make fat babies, Okay?"

"Okay," she said and even managed a little smile.

"Good girl," he said. Then he rose and called Gregor to leave off Nicky's corpse. They'd get to that later. As they walked out, Stanis turned back to Layla. "We go now to look for this Bruno. Thank you for your help. I am sorry about Nicky, you know. Sometimes the shit happens. To all of us."

And then they were gone and Layla was alone again. Well, alone again except for the big wooden cable wheel with Max stuffed inside.

She waited until the Ivans had been gone a while, just to be sure it wasn't some kind of trick. Then she helped him into her car and back to the *Mercy* where she'd stashed the duffles in his room. She gave him his cut and would have taken him to the hospital but he wouldn't go. He had a delivery to make.

She sat outside, watching the goings on in the house though the big front window. These people didn't believe in bars apparently.

There was Mrs. Housefire and there was a tall straight-laced guy who just had to be Mister. And there was the little boy, Terrance, bubbling around the place, happily jabbering about something the way kids

246

do. It was a good life for somebody. Not for her but for somebody. They were lucky.

Eventually she went down and knocked.

"Where's Max?" said Reggie.

"Not here," said Layla. "You gonna ask me in. It looks like rain again."

Reggie didn't move. Okay. Fine. Layla shoved the brown paper bag at her.

"What's that supposed to be?"

"That's Max's cut," she said. "Yours, I mean."

"Max's cut of what?"

"You had a deal, right?" said Layla. "Ten K and he gets to see his son."

Reggie took the bag, clearly not really believing a word until she looked inside. She was speechless for a second then and, when she looked up, she wasn't quite the hard girl she'd been. Even with the scar she was a lot softer.

"How come it's you bringing it?" she said.

"He asked me."

"That's all?"

"Yup," said Layla. "That's it. It's what he wanted. It's the right thing."

"You sound like him."

"Think so, huh?"

"Don't fall for it," said Reggie.

"Fall for what?"

"That whole Square-Jaw-Do-the-Right-Thing shit he's slinging. Think I don't know? Think I ain't been right where you are?"

"Honey," said Layla with more edge than she intended. "You got no clue where I am right now."

"That's what he does," said Reggie, her mouth

twisting into something between a grimace and a smile. "He gets up under you and fucks everything up."

"Probably too late for that," said Layla. She threw a glance at the house looming behind the other woman, all warm and homey, and shrugged. "And it looks like you did okay for yourself."

"What's that supposed to mean?" said Reggie, steeling up again.

"It means what it means," said Layla, starting back towards the street. "You got the house. You got a guy who loves you. You got the kid. Pretty soon you're gonna get your face back. You might want to think about cutting Ol' Max some slack."

Then she was down the steps and gone.

She took him to the hospital, listed as his wife even though she could tell none of the staff believed her. She figured they let it slide because nobody should have to sit in those antiseptic, impersonal rooms alone. Or maybe it was the fat lump of cash she dropped on the admittance desk when she hauled him in.

They assured her he'd be fine– a little cleanup surgery, a short rehab and fine. The news made her feel something she hadn't in, well, maybe never.

Was she happy? Is that what this was?

As she sat there watching him sleep off the drugs they'd pumped into him for the work they did on his jaw, she found herself drifting back to that last sunny day with Jumper.

Him and his idiot surfer friends had spent the day fighting waves and Bennies trying to slide into their territory.

"Locals Only, bitches," Jumper would say, before he and the boys went from happy-go-lucky mooches to delivering the worst kind of ass-kicking an amateur could hand out.

This time the Bennies, some chollo kids from the other side of the city, hadn't pushed them to a fight and everything had ended with smoking BBQ, killer boom box tunes and a sunset that looked like something by Maxfeild Parrish.

Jumper hung his arms on her like she was part girlfriend and part property, like he was, just by touching her, saying, "This is my territory too. Locals only."

It was the first and last time she'd accepted that from a guy without wanting to put steel between his ribs. It was the last time

she remembered feeling happy. Until now.

I fucking hate you, Max, she thought with a cozy kind of rue. *You did this to me.*

Maybe Mrs. Housefire was on to something with all that settle- down, sitcom stuff. Maybe. Or maybe she didn't know a good thing when she saw it the first time and she'd been sucking down a diet of sour grapes and crow ever since. Maybe.

She knew hanging around was a mug's play. The Ivans would track down Bruno sooner rather than later. They were monsters but they weren't idiots. They'd put it all together and she had to be far from the Harbor, looking like someone else and answering to something other than Layla before they did.

Maybe she'd start using her real name again; that would be a nice change. Then again, going back to basics was too big of a turn. Those clothes might still be too small.

Maybe it wasn't time just yet.

She pulled the word *Marisol* from somewhere and rolled it around in her mind. It was a good name, simple and pretty and, if she wanted a clean break, her money would go a lot farther for a lot longer if she skipped way south for a while. And she could unload the Snow fast in TJ or even Ciudad Mier.

She got another flash, this time of Carlos teaching her Spanish with sex and grapes on the Miami sand. She smiled. It had been a long time since she'd been in the sun. That thing in the Harbor's sky was as gray as the name.

She would be in the sun again. She'd bake herself as brown as Max and dance and fuck and...

Max stirred in his cotton sheets, grumbling about something dreamy, drawing her back to the world again. Her hand was on his forehead, stroking gently, settling him again, before she realized she'd put it there.

Soon as he wakes up, she told herself, watching his chest rise and fall. *Soon as he's thinking straight, I say my good-byes and zoom.*

It was another day and night and still, for some reason, she couldn't get through the door of the little white room. She found herself asking him if he wanted her to wait a bit longer, because, maybe, well, if he was up to it...

"Nope," he'd said when she'd offered him the choice of Harbor or Highway. "I ain't trying to leave my boy, now I know he's in the world."

She asked him about the Ivans. He laughed and obviously regretted it.

"They ain't got shit on me. Don't know me from a cool breeze."

He had a point. She didn't. He reminded her, for the third time, the trail would lead to her eventually if she let it.

"I need to go," she said. "I really need to go."

"Yeah," he said. "You do."

On the fourth day she still hadn't and she didn't know why. The little white room was safe– for both of them, for now. Outside was the world, gray and cruel and made, as far as she had ever been able to tell, entirely of sharp teeth.

For now, just for the few moments they'd been able to squeeze out, this little room was the one place no one who knew her could find her. Which meant no one, really; she'd made dead certain of that. 'Layla' was as fictional as the love she'd shared with the late Nikolai Rushkoff. Anybody looking for Layla would find an empty space.

Max slept for a lot of it– painkillers– and only ate what they brought him, sometimes sharing with her. It was at those times she first thought he'd actually looked at peace, like a real person instead of something you chisel out of rock and set in the garden to scare off the animals.

They were both safe in the little white room– safer inside the soft moments. But the hospital's protection had a timer on it and that clock was ticking.

It struck her, sitting, watching him breathe there, that this room was like the one in her head and not just because it was white.

She could see the city out there through the little

window, all grey and black shadows.

It actually looked cold what with the last clinging scarlet leaves being flicked off branches by an increasingly vicious wind.

Every building she could make out looked on the verge of shivering. It was like Winter had had enough waiting, enough rain and fog, and was giving Autumn the Bum's Rush.

She hugged herself in sympathy for it and suddenly remembered an interview she'd read in one of the celebrity rags about some English band touring US cities.

The lead singer chick had said something about dying places being like animals and how some of them could suck you down with them as they slid into the dark.

It had sounded like bullshit to her then, just one more fake philosopher trying to spew some ten-cent deepness for the microphone, but now, looking at the Harbor from the outside, she got it.

So, get the hell out, Snow Queen, she thought. *What the fuck is keeping you?*

"Working on them vacation maps yet?" he said to her back. There was a little bit of a lisp from how they'd wired his jaw; he'd keep that for another few weeks. The rest of him was mostly done healing. Tough bastard. No shock there.

She slid into the chair beside his bed and gave him her version of smile. It had been a long time since she'd used those muscles the proper way, the way where it meant what it actually meant. She hoped it landed right.

"Been thinking about the beach," she said. The

words came out slow and soft as if through a sieve.

"The beach?"

"Yeah," she said, staring again out into the grey. She could just make out the dim contours of the waterfront, dark beneath the lighter sky- in the distance. "Ever been?"

He laughed. "Desert don't count, I guess," he said.

"Not so much," she said. One of the little tugs that helped guide the freighters in when they brought goods from Canada chugged along the dark expanse belching even darker smoke into the air. "The beach. Hot sand. Cold, clean water. Happy people."

"What beach?" he said and it sounded like he was really interested. Shocking.

"Doesn't matter," she said. "Everybody's got a favorite. I just was thinking, y'know, people have been going in and out of that water for like, ever. Swimming. Drowning. Having sex. Playing. Forever."

"Okay..."

"It's like, if you step in it, you're stepping into the same thing some guy way back in the Roman times did or some movie star in the fifties or something like that. Like touching them. Like you're connected to them and they're connected to you."

"I never been to the beach," he said.

"And then I thought, but it's different too. Like it's never really the same ocean. Not really. It's like it changes and it doesn't."

"Yeah," he said. "I guess I can see that. I guess."

"I want to do that," she said. "I want to be like that."

She watched his reflection in the glass as he shook his head, obviously not getting it. He grimaced as he shifted, putting stress on his stitches.

"So you're going south," he said through his teeth.

"Somewhere, yeah," she said, soft and close.

For some reason she felt talking to him had to be private from now on, intimate; there was a duty nurse lurking around out there and this was none of her business.

"Last chance. You sure you don't want to come?"

"Nah," he said, grunting as he tried and failed to get up on one elbow. She moved in on him and without asking, helped him settle back into the mattress. He accepted her hands without bucking. They'd come that far, at least. "I done all the traveling I'm gonna."

"You can take the boy out of the Harbor," she said with a rueful smile.

"Yeah," he said. "Something like that."

"Gonna push the dad thing, huh?" she said. "That's locked in?"

"Locked and loaded," he said. Typical.

She watched as his thumb mashed the morphine dispenser and was happy to see his face soften as the drug took hold. He was holding enough pain on her account. She didn't enjoy having to actually see him do it.

"You should get ghost, ASAP," he said eventually. "You already gave them Ivans too much time to run you down."

"Not a problem," she said.

"No," he said with a hint of his normal force. "I'm thinking: They gotta end up getting next to that one chick you know. From the diner. Soon as they talk to her-"

He trialed off in favor of more morphine but his eyes stayed open and fixed on her.

"Don't worry about me, Max," she said, letting her real face show, letting him see the steel and intelligence behind her eyes for the first time. For some reason it was important to her that he know, just a little bit, what she was underneath. "It ain't good for you."

He laughed, obviously hurting himself.

"No shit," he said. "Last time I did that, look what happened."

They both smiled at that and she let it be quiet between them for a few moments before she said she was sorry for all of it.

She could see from the expression on his face that he was shocked to hear that from her. So was she.

"Don't sweat it," he said.

"No," she shot back, suddenly hot and not knowing why. She could feel herself flushed, feel her voice getting louder, feel her hands clenching tight as if they knew she needed them to be fists. "You don't say that. You don't just blow it off like it's just something people do."

"Look, Layla," he clearly meant to say something, the right something, damn him, but she couldn't let him. She knew if she stopped, she wouldn't get it out and it had to get out for some reason. She had to say this, to him, now, or never. She didn't want never; not for this.

"I know people," she said. "They're shitty. What you did for me, people don't do that. You do. Just you. So I *am* sweating it, okay, Captain America? I am FUCKING sweating it."

"Okay," he said, sounding like one of those animal activists you saw on the RESCUE NETWORK when they were talking some terrified but deadly predator into quiet. "Okay, easy. I'm just saying, 'it's okay,' okay? You did what you had to do. Like you said, I'm in your shoes, maybe I do it that way too."

"God damn," she said, trying not to sob or shriek. "It's just that easy for you, ain't it? Jesus Christ!"

"It ain't," he said. "Never was. What put me here is me. I stepped over the line. I got paid. Nothing to do with you."

"Nothing to do with me?" she said, her face actually flushing red from anger.

"I'm just telling you," he said. He obviously had no idea what this storm was about but he wanted it to pass quick. "You got nothing to be sorry for."

"God damn," she said. "Mrs. Housefire wasn't kidding. You are fucking relentless." She was barely holding it in, whatever it was. She was holding it back with just her fingernails and she could see on his face that Max was afraid it would break her into pieces before she shoved it down again. She was afraid too. "Listen."

"I hear," he said.

"Then, hear this, okay," she said. "I don't feel sorry, Max. You get me? Not me. I don't feel fucking sorry. Not for me, not for you, not for anybody."

He just watched her, his eyes quiet and deep. He didn't say anything but she could see it all over his face what he thought; *Sure, you don't, kid. You go on running that line. Maybe you'll even believe it some day.*

She knew that's what he thought and, for a second,

it made her want to stab him.

She felt her fingernails digging into her palms as she clenched her hands into two tight fists.

"I'm looking at you," she said, her voice gone soft and low as she tried to wrap what she was feeling around the words, inadequate as they had to be. "I'm looking and all I can see is what you did, for me."

"For you?" he said, still quiet, still watching her with that look, that fucking *look*.

"Oh, I know you'll say it was for the money," she said. "But you know that's a lie. You did it because you wanted to help me. A fucking stranger. You're the first person in a long time. Shit, you're the *only*. And what I did, to you, I mean what I almost did, I mean, I'm, I'm just, I'm just so-"

She shattered. All she was for the next five minutes was tears on his chest and long, body-wracking sobs that climbed up out of her from somewhere so deep she had forgotten it was still in there.

She felt his hand on her, his fingers running through her hair, back and forth, so gently, the way you would an inconsolable child when words were useless. She was surprised at how little like rock they felt.

Then, when she was done, she lay there on top of him, sharing her heat with his, using him like an anchor to hold her in place as the world swirled around her for a few seconds more.

"All right, then," she said at last, lifting off of him.

"All right, then," he said.

"So, I'm going," she said, hefting her duffel onto her shoulder, happy to sag a little under the weight of all that cash and snow.

"Shoulda been gone," he said. "I been telling you."

"Yeah." She glanced outside at the gray city with the gray name.

Yeah, she thought. *All done. Time to go.*

"Can't say it was nice meeting you," he said.

He didn't force a grin this time but she could hear it in his voice.

"Nope, you can't," she said, smiling. "'Cause you never did."

He closed his eyes, wincing slightly from the slice of pain the drugs allowed to slip through.

When he opened them again there was a stack of hundreds on the little side table, about 5k worth.

Layla was gone.

•••

Someone was playing music somewhere, just beyond the drapes. It was something old, he could tell that much, a little bluesy, a little jazzy, nice, sexy.

Some sister was singing about how hard the world was in the old days and she wasn't kidding. Same old song. He couldn't pick out the words but the tune lay down beside him like a lover because that's how they did it back then.

His eye strayed back to the window and the city beyond. The clouds were threatening rain again– a big one by the look of them. They were thick and dark, rolling down over the city like chubby pole dancers at the end of a shift. Good.

For the first time in his life he was glad for the rain. There would be a couple more weeks of big storms blowing in off the lake.

After that it would all be snow, a desert of clean white covering everything until the spring came to

258

melt it and all the frozen ghosts away. He smiled, catching his own broken reflection in the glass.

Hell of a pair, he thought and then, *all three of us.*

The Harbor was a million ghosts and a million memories all piled on each other but it wasn't the place he knew anymore.

It didn't know him either, if it came to that.

The years had made them strangers and, in a way, he was glad. If nothing in the Harbor was really the same maybe it meant he didn't have to be either.

His ghosts had been riding him long enough.

That's all they were good for anyway, right, haunting, filling up your head with old weight and dust.

He'd had enough of that.

It was time for something new.

ABOUT THE AUTHOR

Geoffrey Thorne was born in the United States and currently lives in Los Angeles, California.

Thorne is currently a writer-producer on the hit TV series, LEVERAGE as well as having written for LAW & ORDER: CRIMINAL INTENT, BEN 10: ULTIMATE ALIEN and the upcoming BEN 10: OMNIVERSE.

His work has been nominated for GLYPH and GENESIS awards and he was a multiple silver medalist in the STRANGE NEW WORLDS short story contests as well as a finalist in the prestigious WRITERS OF THE FUTURE AWARD.

Thorne is the co-founder and writing partner of GENRE 19, a studio he formed with visual artist Todd Harris in 2008 and the founder and EIC of THE WINTERMAN PROJECT.

"The simple truth is I spend a lot of time thinking up stories about weird things. I'm never really happy sticking solidly in a single genre. I like to mix Romance with Horror, Science Fiction with Noir and everything with some Fantasy. The point is to tell a fun yarn and take the reader somewhere they hadn't thought to go."